THE LIGHT IN HER DARKNESS

CLARA WHITESTONE

Contents

CHAPTER 1

The glow of a white light as pure as snow veiled my vision, its beauty and lack of decadence leaving a mark of perplexity behind.

With its streaks so blinding, there was a strange sense of familiarity embodying it, yet I was left behind its fog.

What is it... about this light... that leaves me feeling warm, yet... cold..?

"Angelica, Angelica."

The echoing of a familiar classmate's voice bounced in the back of my mind, and I unconsciously blinked those feelings away.

I smiled sweetly and responded with a soft "yes?", despite his scorn.

A corner of Nathaniel's lips quirked upwards into an insidious smirk while he leaned closer.

"Don't you find it ironic how your name means 'angel'? I mean no one thinks you're pretty. You wear the ugliest clothing, and you always have your hair in that pony tail of yours."

His hand reached for my pony tail, threatening to tear it off.

"You could be so much prettier if you would just let your hair down once in a while."

"And buy actual clothes that actual teenagers would wear." Nathaniel's friend, Cameron, added.

I lowered my eyes at what I was wearing as my smile started fading away slowly. I knew I didn't wear what others would wear, but that's because what all the other girls wore were very tight clothing, and they always showed too much skin. It was unsafe and disrespectful, and God would frown upon it. I felt the fuzzy fabric of my long sleeve shirt that had a kitten on it, and then my eyes wandered to my dark blue jeans, prior to my eyes re-fixating on Nathaniel and Cameron.

My lips separated as I spoke with an earnest smile. "I wouldn't want to change myself just to please others..." I then tightened my ponytail, realizing it was getting loose. "You like football. And that's great. It's what you like, and if it makes you so happy, if it puts a smile on your face, who cares what others think about it?" My smile widened as I gained back the spark in my ocean-blue eyes.

"So you don't care what anybody thinks of you?" He snarled in disgust and confusion.

"No." I voiced, sweetly.

And, it was true. I didn't care what others thought about me. Did you think that was the first time someone had told me my outfit was ugly, or that I was ugly? Because it wasn't. In fact, I got this sort of thing every day... and usually from the same people. But, I had never let it get to me, because I knew deep down that they had a heart and that somewhere in that heart was a soul. A human being. And every human being cared... just expressed it in different ways.

For Nathaniel, he expressed his humanity through degrading everyone's appearance.

But, he didn't know better. He didn't know how much destruction he could cause by his harsh words. He was just an ignorant boy lost in his own little fantasy world. He couldn't know better. And, I worried for all of those who were actually affected by those words. I even wanted to protect them somehow... someway, but I knew that I, out of all people, could do nothing about it. I was tiny and too soft spoken. And, I knew that I just didn't have it in me to do anything. I was too shy, and he wouldn't take me seriously. I mean, how could I have stood up for anyone when I couldn't even stand up for myself?

I just had to accept the fact that good things couldn't exist without the bad.

Nathaniel smirked and let out a hysterical laugh. At that point, all of my classmates had directed their stares at the three of us. This wasn't new though. We practically went through this routine everyday as if it were rehearsed.

"Can you believe this girl?" Nathaniel directed his focus on Cameron now. Cameron just laughed along with him, leaving me in my own silence.

Just then, someone stepped their foot into the classroom- a woman. But, no one noticed, or no one seemed to care. They just continued talking and laughing among one another, not sparing a glance towards the front of the room.

"That guy over there is hot." One girl said, pointing at Jack, one of the kids everyone seemed to idolize.

"He wants you," another presumed. "You're a cheerleader. He's a football player. What a perfect match!"

"Yea, Claire. You have to go talk to him after class. He's been eyeing you for quite some time now. You've got to give it a try."

Claire was also popular as you could see. And, her friends were right. They would be the perfect couple. Claire was the captain of the cheer-leading team along with being one of the leaders of the National Honors Society, and Jack was the team captain of the football team along with being the smartest in Robotics. He could practically make anything he wanted to, which made everyone intrigued.

They were the two most popular kids in school, so they were bound to be together forever. If Jack was going to date anyone, Claire would have been the only fit. She would had been the only one worthy.

Realizing I was disrespectfully ease-dropping in their conversation, I shifted my eyes to look at the woman who then set her case down on her desk. She must had been the new teacher. We'd been having subs for the past couple of weeks because the old teacher found a better teaching job somewhere else and quit in the middle of the school year.

She glanced around the room, noticing all of the chaos. Everyone was yelling at one another, most enjoying themselves, but some yelling out of anger and rage. She had the lightest blue eyes, and I witnessed them when they had found mine. She tilted her head in what had seemed to be out of curiosity.

She must had been wondering why I was the only one who was calm and eager to learn. Her gaze never looked away, so I started feeling uncomfortable in my own skin. No one ever looked at me for this long. They usually just took a quick glance, if any, and then turned away. But, she didn't do that.

Maybe she was wondering why I would have the courage to wear such an outfit.

I gulped, shyly, and turned away, looking at the floor instead of the woman.

She recognized my nervousness and shook her head as if trying to break out of the trance she was in.

"Ehem." She cleared her throat. "Ehem." She made her voice louder so that everyone could hear her.

The classroom immediately became silent as their eyes finally landed on her. I then focused my eyes back on hers, though I felt my insides tossing and turning just by looking at her. And, it was such an overwhelming feeling because I had never experienced it before. It felt as if someone had grabbed my heart out of my chest and had shattered it. It was such an unbearable feeling, and I wondered what made me feel such a feeling.

"My name is Ms. Hale." She spoke softly, as she wrote on the board.

"What the hale?" Someone almost immediately joked, receiving a high-five from his friend, who was beside him.

Another feeling that I've never experienced before attacked me... attacked my heart. My eyes unintentionally sent darts at him as my mind screamed at his rudeness.

Ms. Hale seemed to not mind the student's joke, probably just because she wanted for them to warm up to her since she was new. But, she shouldn't have just let everyone walk all over her.

"Very funny." She smiled sweetly at the kid, which made the kid feel embarrassed. I guess he didn't expect for her to be so lighthearted about it. My smile returned to my face.

"I know." He said, gaining his confidence back with a smirk plastered across his face.

Ms. Hale paid no attention to his devious smirk though. Instead, she picked up a few sheets of paper and placed it on everyone's desk, prior to telling us to fill it out so that she could see what we knew already.

I watched as she handed the paper out, but when she got to my desk, she gave me a smile as she handed it to me, rather than just placing it on my desk. Our hands had brushed for about a second. Startled, my hand flinched at the encounter, and I dropped the assignment.

She looked at me with worried eyes, probably wondering why I had reacted the way I did.

"I-I'm sorry..." I stuttered.

I rose up, out of my seat, and reached for the paper that had dropped.

Ms. Hale's hand reached for it too, and once again, her hand sent electricity through mine, which made me drop it once more.

My cheeks immediately reddened. I felt so embarrassed, and I had no idea what was wrong with me today. It was so unlike me to act so strange and to feel so strangely around anyone.

So, why is this happening to me now?

"Aha." She chuckled a bit as she grabbed my hand and placed the paper in between my fingers.

I tried with everything in me to ignore my foreign feelings and to accept the assignment from my nice teacher. I didn't want to drop it again. My classmates were already starting to stare at me.

I never did like the attention.

I then heard a familiar voice, which made my heart frown.

"Really Angelica? I knew you were a cluts, but you're dropping paper too?" Nathaniel started to unleash a powerful laugh as his words made me feel even more embarrassed than I already had.

I bowed my head down as Ms. Hale looked at Nathaniel and then back at me, her eyes filled with concern.

"Detention!" Ms. Hale chastised.

"Y-yes ma'am..." I nodded my head, accepting my fate.

She just looked at me confused. "No. Not you. Why would I give you attention when you're the victim?" I'm... the victim?

Her eyes became fiery as they shifted to Nathaniel. Her voice also shifted- back to stern- which scared me a little. She seemed too nice of a person to be capable of speaking like that.

"What is your name?"

"Nathan." He gulped. I could see how frightened he was.

"Nathan, I'll be seeing you after class for detention."

"Okay..." He silently cursed.

Still on the floor, I held onto my knees as I felt everyone's eyes on Nathan and I. I wanted more than anything for this class to end already, but we still had about twenty minutes left.

"And, you..." I heard Ms. Hale's soft feminine voice as she kneeled down to match my height. She then placed a hand on my knee. "Are you okay?"

I nodded my head, never looking at her. I figured it would just be easier to look at the ground.

She then got up, off of the floor, and grabbed my backpack. I lifted my head and watched her as she did so. What is she doing?

"Follow me, Angelica."

My name rang in my ears as a minuscule smile played on my lips, my embarrassment dissipating a little.

She remembered my name.

No one ever remembered me. At least, not the real me.

All throughout my life, I had been harassed and bullied, but that's because no one understood me. I was the only devoted and declared Christian in this school, and so, automatically, I was different and discriminated upon. And, I guess you could say that I basically shut everyone out. I didn't want to become too close to anyone because, every time I found myself too attached, I got disappointed. I would always be let down.

No one cared about me, and so, in response, I became reclusive. I kept to myself and never wanted to let anyone in. Not again.

Though Ms. Hale didn't know me yet, I felt very close to her already. I felt a sense of security around her. No one had ever tried to defend me before, but here she was, putting Nathaniel in his place for me.

She protected me.

And, hearing her say my name on her lips... I never thought I would be so happy to hear it.

I followed her to Daryl's seat. He was the guy who had cruelly joked around earlier. I felt my hands curling up into fists as I had wondered why she would lead me there.

"You'll be switching seats with Angelica from now on." Ms. Hale stated, giving Daryl no choice in the matter.

Gathering what was happening, I spoke up with the little bit of confidence I had.

"Y-you don't have to do that..."

"No, Angelica. I must." She insisted.

I smiled as I answered the last question of the assignment. It was not that hard. Literature has always been my strongest subject.

Soon after, the bell rang and everyone left the room except Nathan and I.

"Angelica." I heard my name close by. I tilted my head up, seeing that my teacher was standing over me, and I blushed. I didn't even hear the bell. "You don't have to stay here."

"I know." I smiled nervously. "Sorry. I wasn't even paying attention."

She smiled as she placed her hand on my assignment. "May I?"

I nodded my head as she lifted it in her hands and started scanning it with her eyes. Her eyes widened as she continued reading the short response section of the assignment, and then a silent laugh escaped her pink lips.

I felt butterflies in my stomach. I thought I was going to throw up. Once again, I was being ambushed with these bizarre... feelings? I didn't know what they were exactly at the time. All I knew was that I didn't like it... and being around Ms. Hale seemed to trigger it within me.

Suddenly, it became a lot harder to breathe than I had remembered. Had I really forgotten how to breathe? Who forgets something so vital? I started panicking, due to my internal predicament, as I watched Ms. Hale getting closer to the end of it.

"Please hurry. I might die before you finish," I had thought.

At that very moment, I honestly believed that to be true. But, in my defense, there was something about her that made my whole body and... mind... do all sorts of weird things. I then came to a conclusion.

She was killing me.

Ms. Hale finally finished my paper and stared at me down, her smile only growing.

"Angelica, you are such a beautiful writer, and your word choices are so exquisite."

I bit my lower lip and closed my eyes, trying to focus on slowing my heart rate.

"Seriously, Angelica. You should be the one talking in class. You have more useful input than half of this class combined."

I curved my lips into a smile. Did she really think I was that smart? She actually liked my writing? I let out a small laugh as I thanked her graciously.

"Thank you, Ms. Hale..."

I stood up out of my seat and placed my paper on top of the stack on her desk, with all of the others. Ms. Hale watched me do this, waiting for me to continue.

"I appreciate your praise... but it's unnecessary."

She sighed as confusion had struck her. I guess she didn't expect me, or anyone, to reject a compliment like that. But, I couldn't just accept it when I was no better than the rest.

"Angelica-"

"I'm just average..." I gave her a smile, a real one, as I put one foot out the door. But, before leaving, I turned my head to look at her one last time. "But, thank you."

"Your welcome..." She seemed a bit baffled over this encounter, so I clarified.

"No one's taken this much interest in me. I only just met you and you've already shown that you care."

"It's my job." She informed me.

I shook my head, not accepting her answer. I continued to look into her icy blue eyes.

"No... not this. It's your job to care about the student... but you..."

She smiled as if she knew what I was about to say, but how could she when I was still figuring it out myself?

A glimmer of a smile crossed my lips as I had recollected my thoughts. "...you care about me as a person."

CHAPTER 2

The smile I had quickly turned into a frown as I reached my house after having walked for ten minutes from the school.

There was a car parked in my driveway, which meant by dad was home.

Why was he here now? He should have been at work for about two hours longer.

I felt shivers running down my spine as my horrid memories had resurfaced through my mind.

Images from the past soared through my thoughts as if I were reliving them. I never knew when I would see the light again.

Remember when I said that everyone cared but expressed their caring in different ways?

Well, Daddy did too...

For him, beating me mentally and physically showed that he cared about me.

I used to hate him for every scar he marked on my body, for every bruise he claimed, for every nasty word he spoke, but now... now I just acknowledge that we all dealt with our love and admiration in different ways.

I couldn't just hate him.

He was all that I had.

I snuck into the house and quietly tip-toed into my room, trying not to make a sound. I didn't want him to know I was at the house just yet.

I closed the door as fear grew inside of me.

"What if he sees me and gets even more mad at the fact that I was sneaking around him like this?" I thought.

I didn't know what was worse. The sneaking and lying, which hurt my soul tremendously, more than words could express, or the fact that instead of greeting me with a smile, he would go right towards the spatula with a devilish grin plastered onto his face.

Both hurt me so much.

I decided that I could just avoid this battle completely by just getting out of the house. I didn't know where to go, but I figured I could just walk around and figure it out.

With that resolve, I walked into my closet and pulled out a sweater, after pulling the other one over my head. I then walked in front of the mirror, which was next to my bed, and I looked into it.

I had scars all over my body, mostly from around my waist and right under my breast. One ran down my back.

I sighed as I looked at my flawed body in the mirror. It just further distanced myself from the others. Everyone had nice slim bodies, and no one was afraid to go into pools and all. But... I was terrified. I was terrified of what people would say when they would see my body and all of its imperfections.

I was scared.

So, lately, as the scars seemed to grow, I began to wear more and more sweaters, even throughout the hot weather.

I slipped my plain red sweater over my head and stared at my now dressed-self, examining my neck and shoulders for any bruises and scars I might have missed.

I didn't seem to find any, so I smiled in success and searched for my wallet.

After about five minutes, I had a mini-panic. I couldn't find my wallet anywhere though I only ever had it in one spot. I checked underneath the cushion of my bed once more, but there was no sign of it.

It was gone.

My heart stopped for a moment as a tear stroked my face, marking my defeat. I worked so hard for that money during my summer job. How could I have been so careless?

I silently sobbed into my hands for what seemed to be eternity, but my whimpering stopped and my head rose as a familiar voice was heard from downstairs.

"Hi, Mr. Rose." A sweet feminine voice greeted my father. Ms. Hale.

My eyes widened as I poked my head out, seeing her at my doorstep. Why was she here? And, how did she know where I lived?

I couldn't help but smile at the pleasant surprise, however.

"What can I do you for?" He asked, seemingly unhappy that Ms. Hale interrupted him doing who knows what.

Ms. Hale seemed unamused but continued with a smile, which seemed forced.

"Is Angelica here?"

I felt my chest drop as I heard her wondering where I was. We weren't at school, and she seemed impressed with me, so I really had no clue what her intentions were.

"Do you hear her anywhere?" He hissed, which made Ms. Hale seem a bit uncomfortable.

I felt my hands curl up into fists as they did before, my blood boiling within me. He would speak to me like this all of the time, but talking to my sweet kind-hearted teacher with no respect was not okay. It just wasn't.

I wanted to make him pay... for everything.

I then shook my head at my own sinful thoughts.

How could I think of such a thing?

He did raise me practically all on his own, so I should be more grateful.

Suddenly, I felt her icy blue eyes find mine. I stayed frozen as I hugged the railing of the stairs. I was on my knees however and my dad's back was facing me, so I knew he wouldn't be able to see me.

Ms. Hale quickly shifted her stare from mine to my dad's again.

I gulped as my body suddenly felt heavy and weak. That was the moment. That was the moment my dad would find out about me sneaking around him. It was over before it even began. I should have known I couldn't have run anything past him like this.

But, I was wrong. I couldn't have been any more wrong.

"Okay. Thank you, sir. Sorry for wasting your time."

Ms. Hale gave him another forged smile before leaving out the door. She never once looked at me again.

I heaved a sigh, out of relief. She didn't say anything. It was as if she could see the fear through my eyes. It was as if she knew I was hiding.

It made me wonder.

I crawled back into my room and silently put the covers over me as I lied on my bed.

I stared up at the ceiling above me as I thought over what had happened that day.

The first time I saw Ms. Hale, it was as if her appearance alone could make me forget about all of the wrongs in the world. And, what a lovely appearance did she have with her dirty blond hair in which grew lighter at the tips and her compelling icy-blue eyes that would leave me dazed.

She instantly made me smile- a real one-which I haven't been able to do for a while, it seemed.

There was just something about her that made my heart flutter with delight and... happiness? I wasn't really too sure what that feeling felt like. Again, it was foreign to me. But, I liked the feeling... a lot.

I then remembered how awkward I was in class. Usually, I would keep to myself and say as little as possible to anyone who would engage in a conversation with me, but I would never stutter. I didn't know why then, but she made me nervous. So incredibly nervous, to the point I was uncomfortable in my own skin half of the time.

But, she came to my house. She needed to see me. But, why? I wanted to know what she needed from me. It was killing me.

A few seconds later, I heard a knock on my window, causing my head to jerk up.

I cautiously tiptoed to the window to see who it was. And, to my surprise, it was Ms. Hale.

I lifted the window up, my eyes drowning in concern. "Ms. Hale... I am on the second floor. You could have gotten hurt getting up here..." I managed to say, despite my heart beat quickening.

She just smiled as she put her hands over mine, which had rested on the rim of the window.

"There was a ladder."

I nodded as my eyes shifted to the ladder, then back to her welcoming eyes.

"I see..." I gulped as her stare became intense on me.

It was as if she were seeing right through my soul.

"Well..." I cleared my throat, which only made Ms. Hale release a small giggle. "Why are you here?" I finally asked.

"I need you to come with me."

I watched as she looked around outside as she remained planted on the roof.

"I don't want anyone seeing me up here. Let's talk at my house." She decided.

I nodded, hesitantly, as she helped me climb out of the window and into her arms.

I felt the pulse of her heart beating on my chest, and it gave me a sense of comfort that hers was beating just as fast as mine. The hug didn't last long though, and I found myself getting disappointed that it ended so soon.

I shook my head at the thought.

She's my teacher. I shouldn't be feeling this way towards her.

And, above all, she was a woman.

None of it made any sense. The feelings I had were never anything I had experienced before, but, for some odd reason, it felt as if they were old feelings that had resurfaced again.

It was as if in some alternative universe, her and I met and grew a bond like no other. An inexplicable, yet unbreakable, bond.

It would explain why I never felt this way until our eyes locked onto each other's. It would explain why I was incapable of caring for anyone else on Earth.

It was only her that could unleash those feelings out of me.

But, though her company made my heart sing, it also made my heart frown.

Like I had mentioned before, it was as if she were someone I had lost. The feeling of losing something- something important- surrounded me as I stood near her aura.

A tear crept its way down my cheek as I internally battled with my paradoxical feelings.

I didn't know it then, but that is exactly what happened. I lost something really important, though I swore to her I wouldn't. I swore to her that I would remember, but I didn't.

Some things just can't be changed. Some things are just fate, and you can't change your destiny.

It just left me with a feeling of emptiness. The ultimate feeling of sorrow, because I could feel all of that pain but couldn't remember why that pain occupied my heart.

There's nothing worse than the power of forgetting...

"Make yourself at home."

I smiled, thanking her before looking around.

The apartment was not decorated too much, but you could definitely tell that someone lived there because there was furniture everywhere. But, it was very simplistic looking and classic.

Ms. Hale gave me a glass of water as she sat down next to me on the couch. I accepted it and drank rather quickly.

"I figured you were thirsty." Her cheeks seemed to flush slightly. "We did walk a few miles to get here."

"Yea..."

I placed the glass onto the table in front of us before lifting my eyes to meet hers. I still didn't know why I was here, but I was glad that I was.

"So, why did you want to see me, Ms. Hale?"

"Please, call me Katherine outside of school."

I nodded. "Did I do something wrong, Katherine?"

She shook her head in disbelief, her brief evidence of squeamishness having disappeared as if it had never occurred.

"That's the second time you've asked me that, Angel."

Angel. The nickname rang in my ears, in a sweet echo.

Her eyes suddenly furrowed as she pondered over what she had just said. *And, there goes the flushed look from earlier.*

"Sorry..." She let out a faint laugh. "I just like the name 'Angel' and it slipped out." She covered her mouth, apologetically, before finishing with, "would it be okay if I were to call you that?"

"Wouldn't it be misleading?" I jested, getting more comfortable around her.

"'Misleading'?"

"Yea..." I cleared my throat once more as I confessed to her about what was going on in school. "It's what people are always saying at school. They say that it's 'ironic' that my name is Angelica when I'm not pretty... or dress-"

"Stop."

Ms. Hale's angelic voice cut me off as she grabbed my hands, intertwining her fingers with mine. My hands tingled at her touch.

"You're beautiful, and the way you dress is adorable."

My eyes widened as she then leaned over me. At first, I thought she was about to kiss my cheek, but she didn't. She paused in that direction as if she were thinking about whether it was appropriate or not, but, instead, she wrapped her arms around me.

I smiled from ear to ear at the physical contact. It had been years since I last received a hug from anyone.

Ever since my mom died in a car accident two and a half years ago, my dad's tolerance and love for me changed and resulted in him doing cruel things to me like smacking me around, tugging me by the hair, and compensating my phone now and then so that I wouldn't cry for help from anyone.

Though, he was wrong about the last part. The last thing I wanted to do was drag someone else into my problems and have them worry for me... and attempt to help.

I didn't want anyone to worry about me.

I snapped out of my blank stare at the wall as I realized I was lost in my head again. Ms. Hale sat next to me, her eyes filled with concern, and, in that moment, I knew what she was doing. She didn't even have to say it.

She wanted to help me. The look in her eyes told me it all. But, I couldn't let her.

I couldn't let her get involved in my unfortunate and sad life.

"Angelica..."

I tilted my head up, locking my eyes on hers as I antici-pated on her next words.

"Do you know why I called you here? Do you remember me saying why?"

She seemed as if she wanted me, with all of her heart, to say that I did. But, she was confused. She never said anything.

"You never told me..." I uttered, getting lost in her blue eyes.

"Hmm..."

She looked away for a second, and I could tell she was struggling with something in her head. It was hurting me to see her like this, and it killed me not knowing why.

"Ugh!" I heard her almost yell. Though I knew that her sudden outburst was clearly directed at herself, it shocked me, and so, involuntarily, I jumped off of the couch.

I watched as Ms. Hale knocked over her lamp, a few stacks of paper and a few plates- the sound of the glass shattering sounding an alarm in my ears.

I cried out in pain. Not a physical pain, but an emotional one.

I was so wrong about her.

This whole time she made me feel so happy and safe, but here she was, destroying her own apartment over a confusion.

I was watching my teacher completely lose it.

I slowly backed away from her, my heart racing uncontrollably in my chest.

But then, something changed... her eyes... they seemed to change- like she had just seen a phantom.

Ms. Hale dropped the paper that was once in her hand, and then, I saw a tear sneak its way down her cheek as realization struck her.

She frantically turned around and walked towards me, but I backed up slowly at every step she took.

"Angelica... I'm so sorry..." she cried.

My eyes started to water, matching hers. I didn't know what to say or how to feel.

"I shouldn't have pressured you to remember something that you clearly did not... I mean, I knew you didn't. There was no way, yet I completely freaked out on you."

She tried grabbing my arm, but she missed as I stepped back out of fear.

"You never told me anything."

Another tear, marked with disbelief, ran down my face.

"I'm so sorry." She continued. "Don't be afraid of me."

My heart ached at her words.

"Don't be afraid of me."

It's not that I was afraid of her. At least, I wasn't. It was more like I was confused and terrified of the fact that I was confused. But, more so, she seemed like she had some things she needed to deal with, herself.

She must have had a hard past, which caused her to strike out. I had hoped she would face whatever it was that was bothering her one day and not allow it to continue hurting her.

"I-I'm not afraid... of you." I cried out, still walking to-wards the door.

"Mhmm..." She watched as I backed away slowly from her and reached for the door knob. She shook her head in disbelief at the turn of events.

This was not what either of us had planned.

But, she let me run away from her, instead of persisting in me staying.

Standing in front of my door, my hand hovered over the doorknob, hesitantly, while my brows creased together; my eyes dampening.

Ms. Hale...

My lashes were stained by the evidence of tears.

I had been crying... every since I had left her house... but, now-

Before I could linger any longer in indecision, the door soon swung open, the silhouette of my father's tall and lean figure blocking the entrance.

My dried up tears resurfaced as my sobbing grew in front of him.

His face scrunched up in disgust.

"What's the matter with you, rat? You spoiled punk!"

My tears continued to downpour.

Was this what it felt like to have heartbreak? It feels as though my heart has been squeezed.

If it wasn't for my cloudy gaze, I would have probably noticed the beers behind him over the kitchen counter, or perhaps the fact that his breath reeked of alcohol.

Although, it wasn't until I felt his abrasive grip tightening over my wrist that I knew what was coming next.

I limped into my bed, carrying my weak body. The continuous beating had gotten so bad to the point I could no longer feel the pain. My body was growing more and more numb to it.

I glanced at my appearance once again in the mirror and found a new bruise on my collar bone.

I winced in pain as I lightly printed my fingers over the wound.

Angelica...

It is ironic. Isn't it?

I was beginning to lose sight of what I used to look like- of what the old me had looked like and felt before my life turned upside down. And, I was beginning to wonder: when would an angel come down to save me? I was starting to lose hope, yet I desperately clung over that withering hope inside of me. The hope that God had a plan for me- that it could only get better.

But, how long did I have to wait? How much of this could I handle before I would completely fall apart?

But, again... we can't change our fate, no matter how hard we try.

For the most part...

CHAPTER 3

"Make sure to finish your homework! I want a well-written essay over anything that interests you. This will help me get to know you all better, both, as a writer, and on a more personal level." Ms. Hale instructed.

We all nodded as everyone gathered their things and headed out the door.

I slowly rose up out of my seat and started packing my bag until a low raspy voice startled me.

"Hey... I'm sorry." Nathan apologized, with his head down. "I guess I pick on other kids because I'm insecure, myself, and picking on you makes me feel less bad about those insecurities."

My eyes widened as I stood there, both, in shock and in awe.

"Wow, Nathaniel... I didn't know. I'm sorry that you're having a difficult time, and if you want, we can be friends, and perhaps, I can help you feel better. I'd help you in any way I can."

He let out a laugh in which he couldn't hold in any longer. "You seriously bought that?"

I frowned as I continued to put my papers into my folder.

"Silly of you to think I would apologize to someone like you." As he walked toward the door, he mouthed, "You aren't worth my breath."

I sighed as I slipped my arms through the straps of my backpack. Just when I thought he had actually changed; just when I thought he had matured and opened up his heart, he proved me wrong.

Soon after, I lifted my head and noticed Ms. Hale's eyes on me.

Throughout the entire class period, she didn't once acknowledge that I existed. Unlike class yesterday, where all she seemed to care about was my safety, she couldn't bring herself to express any of that concern today.

She just addressed the class, as a whole, and sat at her desk, buried in one of her books, as we worked on our essays.

She must have felt too ashamed of what happened last night and couldn't convince herself to talk to me. And, I'm not going to lie. It hurt so much because she was the only one in my life that actually showed me that my life was worth anything.

Everyone belittled me and took my kindness and lack of retaliation for granted.

Ms. Hale slowly put her book down and walked over to me, her icy blue eyes concentrating on my sad expression the entire time.

"Angel." She said, in a low voice but above a whisper. "Can you stay after class for a minute?"

Staring into her eyes, I saw her regret and remorse. I squinted my eyes as I gave a small nod.

"Sure, Ms. Hale..." I smiled politely, but she could see the hurt and the dismay in it.

She opened her mouth, attempting to say something more, but then almost immediately closed it.

We both stared at the door as it shut, and then we redirected our stares back onto each other.

We were alone.

"Angelica, about last night..."

She looked at the ground as if she was ashamed of the memory.

"I was so unprofessional and cruel to you... a student. There are no words that could even describe how terribly sorry I am for putting you through all of that, for allowing my emotions to run out of control and for you having to witness that."

I smiled weakly as I instinctively wrapped my arms around her. Not for me, but for her. Though she had scared me, it was evident that she was scared that night also. And, for whatever the reason, though I didn't know then, I wanted to help her.

At first, she just stood there, in shock, barely returning the hug, but later, she tightened her grip around my waist, making me lose my breath.

"T-thank you... Angelica." A hopeful tear ran down her face and onto my shoulder.

My eyes widened, but I didn't look up.

I didn't want to see my teacher cry. She was hurting... so much. But, I didn't know why. It made my heart ache for her. I wanted her to feel happy again.

I knew what true pain felt like. I knew how true sadness could deteriorate your soul.

And, in that moment, I wished that no one would have to go through that kind of pain ever again.

"I didn't expect you to hug me."

She wiped her tears from her face as she unwrapped one of her arms and held my chin in between her thumb and forefinger. She looked into my eyes and gave me a painful smile that made me want to cry, but I held it together.

"I'm supposed to be comforting you, yet you're the one comforting me." She let out the faintest laugh.

Not knowing what had possessed me in that moment, or why I had felt compelled to do so, I traced the outline of

Katherine's jaw, admiring her perfect facial structure... and her.

"I don't want to see my teacher cry." I vocalized, with a confidence I didn't know I had.

She chuckled, lightly. "I must look really pathetic and childish to you right now..." She whined.

"No. You don't, Katherine. You're just being human."

"I'm being a child..." She persisted.

"Okay... maybe you are acting like one," I mocked playfully.

The way Ms. Hale's eyes seem to light up with her laughter she half-hid with her hand made my heart flutter, subconsciously.

"Angelica, was that a joke? Did you just joke around me?" She arched a brow. "When I first saw you, you were so shy. You looked like you would be running away screaming if you weren't required to sit in my classroom."

I blushed a deep red. I was shy. I've always been, no matter who I was around.

But, in that moment, something in me, a part of me that didn't worry, the part of me that I didn't know existed, came out.

She brought it out of me.

"I am shy." I wasn't denying it.

She stared at me intently as if taking mental notes on what I was going to say next.

"But, with you..."

"You bring the best out of me," we spoke in unison.

The coloring in my cheeks deepened as I heard her agree with me.

Whatever this was, whatever was happening between us, it was clear to me then that she felt it too.

It was as if the universe wanted us to meet. But, like this? It was a cruel game we had to play. I was a student, barely over eighteen, and a devoted Christian, yet I was put into a life that didn't fit me... and I was growing too close to someone I barely knew, but shouldn't know on a personal level.

And, no matter how much I longed to have a deep and affectionate connection with someone, I had to remind myself that she was my teacher and that it would be wrong if we were to become friends... or more than that.

I had to let go of what I had searched for, and it broke my heart.

I broke our eye contact as I released her face from my grasp.

She watched my sudden gaze towards the ground before lifting my chin up once more, in order to reconnect my eyes and figure out what I was thinking... or feeling.

"What are you thinking about?"

I bit my lip. A Christian must be honest, but some truths are too hard to say.

"Just that..." I saw my reflection within her dilating pupils.

I want to tell her.

"I should get going."

"To your house?" She presumed.

I felt my body quiver at the thought of being in that house again and with my abusive father.

Though it was my house, I felt very unwelcomed there, and it was the last place I wanted to go to.

My thoughts of last night abruptly and harshly flooded my mind though I tried to forget.

Standing in front of my door, my hand hovered over the doorknob, hesitantly, while my brows creased together; my eyes dampening.

Ms. Hale...

My lashes were stained by the evidence of tears.

I had been crying... every since I had left her house... but, now-

Before I could linger any longer in indecision, the door soon swung open, the silhouette of my father's tall and lean figure blocking the entrance.

My dried up tears resurfaced as my sobbing grew in front of him.

His face scrunched up in disgust.

"What's the matter with you, rat? You spoiled punk!"

My tears continued to downpour.

Was this what it felt like to have heartbreak? It feels as though my heart has been squeezed.

If it wasn't for my cloudy gaze, I would have probably noticed the beers behind him over the kitchen counter, or perhaps the fact that his breath reeked of alcohol.

Although, it wasn't until I felt his abrasive grip tightening over my wrist that I knew what was coming next.

"D-dad, please-"

Dragging me into the house by the hair, he slammed the door behind him before smacking my face, brutally. Luckily, it didn't leave a mark.

I winced in pain, lifting a hand to touch my cheek when he then grabbed my hand, viciously, throwing me into the living room.

I felt my body grow weaker and weaker, and I knew at any moment that I would pass out.

"I know what you were up to."

My eyes started closing, due to fatigue, but I got a glimpse of the shadowy figure approaching me.

"I can't believe you actually tried hiding from me... again! I'm your freakin' father! Show me some respect!"

Rage filled his voice as it heightened after every word he spoke.

"I-I'm sorry... Da-"

I was interrupted by another smack to the face.

I cupped my hands and buried my face in them as tears streamed down, burning my skin.

"Shut up! Don't you dare speak."

"How much more can I take..?" I thought.

Ms. Hale's eyes widened as she pulled me into another hug. My body ached at her touch. I felt very sore.

"Did I just say that out loud?"

I pleaded that I hadn't, but, unfortunately, I did.

"You did..." She stroked my hair, still holding me close to her.

"Is it about your home?"

Releasing me, she soon looked into my eyes, her stare filled with concern.

"Did something happen? Are you hurt?"

I stared silently into her eyes, unable to bring myself to answer.

"You're coming home with me." She finalized.

She picked up her case from her desk and then reached for my hand, which I gratefully took.

"Yes ma'am." It was all I could manage to say.

As I stepped my foot into the now familiar house, I found myself looking for the broken plates, the lamp and the scattered papers, but it was as if it had never happened. She cleaned it up well.

"You can sit down on the couch, sweetie, and we can watch a movie and eat ice cream. How does that sound?"

Though she smiled at me, I could see through that smile. She did it to make me feel more at ease, when, in reality, she was worried about me.

"Sounds good," I softly spoke, ignoring my thoughts.

A few minutes later, after giving me a bowl of ice cream, Katherine Hale opened up a drawer within the table underneath her T.V.

"Okay. Don't judge, but I don't usually watch movies here at my house, so they're mostly older ones."

I grinned widely at her cuteness.

"What do you have?"

"Princess Bride. Um..." She scavenged further. "White Chicks, Mean Girls, Kung Fu Pand-" She cut herself short as her cheeks reddened ever so slightly. "How about we just do Princess Bride? It's a bit romantic... but the story is very heart-warming and fantastic."

I laughed and nodded in approval. "I don't mind."

She slipped the movie into the DVR, and I instantly got intrigued. It was so random, and most of the things couldn't happen, but it ultimately showed how true love could prevail and conquer anything, which made me have hope.

Maybe Katherine and I can-

"Angelica." I heard a whisper, and I turned my head to find Katherine watching me, rather than the movie.

"U-um. Yes?" My shyness returned, and I suddenly felt awkward with her being this close to me.

"How are you liking the movie?"

I could see the excitement in her eyes. Though she made it out like she didn't care for any of the movies she had, she seemed especially thrilled about this one.

I matched her smile and winked after saying, "Oldies rock!"

"Doesn't it though?" She agreed, letting out a light laughter.

"Yea. It's definitely a great movie, but I wish the creators would have made this more realistic."

"You don't like the poison?" She smirked.

"It's not that," I giggled with her. "It's more about the message..."

I scratched my forehead as my smile transformed slightly.

"The movie is really pointing out the impossible. It basically influences the idea that love prevails and can conquer anything, but in real life..." Our eyes met. "...that is just a delusion. Don't you think?"

I didn't know why but, after asking that question, I genuinely wanted to know her answer. I wanted to know how she felt on the matter.

I suddenly wished she would disagree with me, and, to my luck, she did.

"I disagree completely," she stated, wholeheartedly. "True, there will be tough battles and risks down the road... but that's with everything you do in life."

She then leaned in closer and tucked my loose strands of hair behind my ears.

I felt my heartbeat quickening, and I suddenly felt a bit better. It was when she would do things like this, I would feel like the old me again. The happy, carefree Angelica.

"...and I think that when you find your true love, it's worth fighting for. No question about it."

I nodded slowly, trying to comprehend what she had just said, as I felt the warmth of her hands behind my ears. She still had them there, which made me wonder if that was intentional or if she hadn't noticed, herself.

"Y-yea." I finally spoke. "It would be nice to believe that."

CHAPTER 4

I slowly lifted my eyelids and allowed for the light to hit them. I squinted as I tried to remember where I was. The ceiling didn't consist of any stars, unlike my room, and the bed felt different. More cozy.

I soon turned my head while shifting my body so that I lied on my side.

My eyes widened as they lied upon the most beautiful thing- Katherine sleeping. She looked so peaceful and happy.

A big smile crept its way onto my face as I stared in awe. Pure joy overwhelmed me as it suddenly hit me. Ms. Hale, my teacher, truly cared about me. She had my best interest. She saw the hurt in my eyes. She saw the despair in me though usually no one would notice because my forged smiles masked the pain within me.

She saw right through my mask.

Another thought hit me though as my mind started to wake up. I was in my teacher's house, and I slept in her bedroom. I was crossing boundaries that I never thought I would cross. If someone were to knock on that door right now and witness this, it wouldn't look good for us.

And, with what luck, I heard something pressed against the front door. I felt my body cringed as I debated what I should do. Should I ignore it?

I then looked at the sleeping beauty and wondered if I should wake her up. I'd feel more comfortable if she dealt with this. I mean, it was her house. But, the thought of waking her up, and for her to possibly get irritated by me for doing so, overwhelmed me.

I'll just answer it.

I dragged my worn out body to the door and took a deep breath before opening it.

A tall man stood before me.

"Hello there." He greeted me.

I stared into his coconut brown eyes and then downward at the package he was holding.

"This is for you." He handed me the package, which I accepted a bit hesitantly.

"For me?" I questioned. How did he know I'd be here?

"You are Ms. Katherine Hale. Right?" He arched a brow. Oh, well that makes more sense.

"N-no." I laughed lightly. "But-"

Before I could finish my sentence, I felt a presence from behind me, and I heard a feminine voice say, "I'm Katherine Hale." I remained frozen, unable to move, and my shyness returned as my cheeks reddened.

"Ah..." He looked at Katherine, and then to me again, trying to put the two together. "I see." A grin appeared onto his face. "Well, good morning to the both of you. Sorry for stealing it." He smirked playfully.

"You didn't. I should have been awake anyway." Katherine asserted, with a small smile resting on her lips.

I looked at the watch on my hand and noticed that it was eight a.m. School started at seven fifth-teen! I've never been late in my life!

Katherine saw the concern in my eyes and held me close as she waved the man goodbye.

"I hope to see the two of you again, sometime soon!" He spoke before the door closed.

He seemed nice.

Immediately, I released myself from my teacher's grasp,and I put my book bag over my shoulders.

"You aren't planning on going out like that. Are you?" She smirked, watching me struggle.

Katherine placed the package, unopened, on the glass table in the living room, not once letting her eyes leave mine. "What?" I then let my eyes roam my body, and I gasped. "I-I didn't bring any clothes with me... and I don't want to go back to my house just yet. My da-" I then paused, realizing I almost told her my secret. Katherine seemed to be taking notice of my sudden pause, but I continued anyway. "I'll just have to go to school like this..."

"With what? The clothes you wore yesterday?" She shook her head. "No. I won't let you do that. Come with me..."

She grabbed my arm, and I followed her like a lost puppy. I felt the warmth in her hands, and it suddenly gave me a sense of comfort. A smile crept its way on my face, but I didn't want her to see that I was smiling, so I quickly forced it to disappear.

"You can wear something of mine." I watched as Katherine scavenged through her closet.

We were very similar in height, though she was slightly taller than me, and we had a similar body type, so I knew instantly that fitting into her clothes wouldn't be a problem. But her clothes seemed very fancy, and to be honest, none of the clothes she had looked like anything I would wear.

I shrugged as she showed me her collection, which just made her smirk.

"Angelica. You have to choose an outfit..."

Grabbing a v-neck dark blue blouse and fancy black jeans, she then turned to face me again.

"Here," she asserted, handing me the outfit, prior to waving me off with a hand. "Let me see it on you."

"Okay." I gave in, finding my way to the bathroom and slipping the clothes on.

I stared at myself in the mirror, and I couldn't help but smile. I looked... pretty. I actually looked pretty.

My smile quickly faded as fear stole that smile from me. The blouse was too low. My collar bone wasn't hidden enough. My scar was visible. I frantically ran from the bathroom and towards Katherine's closet as I covered my collar bone with my hands.

She furrowed her eyebrows, with a concerned expression on her face.

"Angel..." she spoke. "You look beautiful. Wait, what's wrong? Did you not like the blouse?" She then paid attention to my shaking hand hiding my collar bone. "You don't have to be shy, Angelica." She assured. "Showing a little bit of skin won't hurt."

I blankly stared at her as my hands remained in their position. I then debated whether this was the time to tell her about my scars, my insecurities, but I didn't want her to feel bad for me.

I let out a sigh and slowly let go of my hands as Katherine reached out hers in order to hold onto mine.

Almost immediately, I heard a gasp, but Katherine's expression softened and a small smile crossed her face.

I looked down at the floor ashamed, but Katherine lifted my chin up so that she could see my face.

"Oh Sweetie. That's nothing to be ashamed of." She lightly grazed my collarbone where my scar was.

I winced at her touch, which she noticed, so she drew her hand back, cautiously.

"It still hurts..." I managed to speak, my head redirected at the ground.

She bit her lip. "Did your dad do this to you?" She put the pieces together.

I felt my heart cringe as the memories of my dad invaded my mind. Still lost in thought, I managed to answer her.

"Yes..."

I quickly raised my head, my eyes widening.

"B-but he hasn't always been like this. You see, two and a half years ago, my mom died in a car accident, and ever since, my dad stopped believing in anything good. He stopped attending church, and he isolated himself from the world... including me."

A tear snuck its way down my cheek.

"He needed a distraction from the pain though he would never admit that he had any. He would never grieve in front of me... maybe he never grieved at all. He would abuse me in order to channel and release that anger he had at God for letting his wife die."

Tears were now streaming down my face as my vision blurred.

"Oh, Angelica."

I felt a warm embrace as Katherine wrapped her arms around me, trying to comfort me.

"You are the most pure thing on this earth, and you don't deserve any of that. Your dad's pain is not your fault, Angelica..." I lifted my head up, which was once buried in her chest, and she wiped the tears from my face with her thumb. "...and that incident doesn't justify his behavior."

I nodded as her words brought clarity. She was right. It wasn't justified, but he was still my father, and I had lots of respect for him.

I guess I just held on to the idea of how he was like before. He was so kind, and everyone in the neighborhood loved him. And, he loved me.

I guess there was a part of me that believed that person was still in him... somewhere. A part of me yearned for his awakening, and so I didn't want to retaliate and have him forget who cared about him- I was always there for him.

"Yea... I know you're right, Katherine." I continued. "I just didn't want to believe that I lost my father too..." My eyes swelled with how much I cried. My words stung my heart as it was hard to say. The truest words can sometimes contain the truest pain. Katherine just stroked my hair, allowing me to cry in her arms.

It was the most I had ever cried in my life. All of my hidden feelings and all of that pain that I had buried finally poured out of me. I needed to cry, and I was glad Katherine was there. I was glad she worried for me.

Because lately, it seemed like no one had. Though I told everyone to not, I secretly wanted someone to care deeply about how I was feeling.

I was glad that person had to be Katherine Hale.

We stepped out of Katherine's car and headed towards the principal's office.

I felt my palms moistening as my nerves ran crazy.

Katherine looked at me, and I could see she wanted to grab my hand in that instant, to comfort me, but she resisted the impulse, probably because we were now in school grounds.

"It's okay." She assured. "You won't get in trouble for being a little late."

I nodded though my guilt still ran through me.

"Ms. Hale. What's the meaning of this?" The principal, Mr. Strickland, stared at us coldly as Ms. Hale and I stepped foot into his office. "I had to get a sub for your first two classes..." He then eyed me as he asked what my name was.

"It's A-Angelica." I murmured.

He pulled a file with my name on it soon after. "Aha. And why are you late Ms. Rose." He gave an annoyed smirk. "According to my records, you haven't gotten into any trouble, and you've had a perfect attendance..." his smirk widened as he continued with, "...until now."

I gulped. "I um... I-"

"Mr. Strickland. Pardon my unannounced absent and for Angelica being late to her class, but you must understand, it was for good reason." Katherine interrupted.

"And, what is that?" He snarled.

I looked at Ms. Hale, wondering what she would say next, and I silently prayed she would think of something good to say in order to save us.

A smile played on her lips as an idea, a perfect idea, ran through her magnificent mind.

"You see, I was putting my case in the car, but then, in the corner of my eye, I saw a girl on top of the tree. And so, instinctively, I went over to her and recognized that it was Angelica. I asked her why she was up there when school was about to start, and she told me that there's a cat that's too scared to get down." She took a breath. "She wanted to save it, so I decided to help her." She smiled as she focused her attention on me and then back at Mr. Strickland. "It's like her to want to help anything or anyone. She has a good heart. But, I guess, in a way, I shouldn't have promoted it, since it had caused us to be late, and so I'm sorry for that." She bowed her head down, and I instinctively matched hers.

"No need for that," Mr. Strickland retorted, causing us to slowly lift our heads up to look at him through our eyelashes. "I won't penalize you this one time. But make sure it doesn't happen again." He warned.

"It won't." Katherine assured, smiling from ear to ear.

"And, you..." He directed his attention to me, and I arched a brow, waiting for him to finish. "Can you speak?" He jested. "You've been so quiet." He noted.

Katherine looked at me and put her arm around me, rubbing my shoulder with her thumb. The sudden contact made me smile, and it gave me some of the confidence I needed to respond.

"S-sorry, sir. I don't usually speak that often."

He let out a light laugh. "And, is there anything in particular you want to add to this conversation?"

I thought for a second before answering with "I think Ms. Hale said it all."

Ms. Hale squeezed my shoulder slightly as her smile remained plastered on her face.

"Alright. Now go to your third period." He directed.

"Yes, sir," we spoke in unison.

Finally, it was seventh period, which was AP Literature. "I get to see Ms. Hale again," I thought. That had convinced my lips to smile.

As I walked in the hallway, people stared at me like hawks and murmurs surrounded me. I wondered what they were talking about or why they suddenly seemed to notice me.

I was no longer invisible.

"Good afternoon, Angelica." Ms. Hale smiled while greeting me at her door.

"G-good afternoon, Ka-" I cleared my throat. "-Ms. Hale." Why was I suddenly so nervous around her again? Just looking at her made my skin crawl. My nerves ran wild, and I began to miss how I felt earlier- when I felt comfort at hearing her voice or when she would touch my hand.

Her smile only widened as her eyes sparkled with delight. She had to have noticed me being suddenly nervous in this encounter. She had to.

I gave a shaky smile as my cheeks reddened, and I sped-walked to my desk.

Everyone's eyes darted at me as ah's and ooh's sounded throughout the room.

I gulped as I pulled out my folder and my black-inc pen, ignoring their astonished eyes.

"Whoa. Is this real?" Nathaniel's eyes examined me up and down. "Are my eyes just playing tricks on me right now?"

"W-what are you t-talking about?" I questioned.

Nathaniel smirked. "You actually look... nice."

My eyes widened. "Did you just compliment me?" It was not like him.

Ms. Hale smiled at her desk as she watched our conversation intently. "I guess I did!" He laughed hysterically, which made my stomach spin. "Cameron." He turned to his friend. "Look at Angelica!"

Cameron bit his lip as his eyes laid upon me. "Girl, I was right. You would be hella cute if you would just wear normal clothes. Now keep it up!" He winked.

I smiled nervously as I glanced upon what I was wearing. It was the clothes I was a bit hesitant to wear. It was Ms. Hale's clothes.

"Thanks," I let out before getting lost in Katherine's eyes, who had already had her eyes on me.

"Alright, class." Katherine walked around her desk and stood in the front. "For those of you who still have your essays, I will take them up now."

I heard lots of whining and moans as some of the students clearly didn't finish.

"One more day, Ms. Hale. That's all I need!" One pleaded.

Ms. Hale sighed as her hand pressed against the paper that lied on his desk.

"I'm sure your essay is fine. After all, we had time in class yesterday for you all to work on them, and it wouldn't be fair if I only gave you the extra time, when everyone had the courtesy to finish in time." She remarked.

The boy frowned as he let go of his grip on his paper. "Yes ma'am." He pouted.

A few desks later, she appeared in front of me, and her eyes locked onto mine. I handed her my essay, never letting my eyes wander away from the sight of her.

"I hope you like it." I bit my lip as I waited for her response.

She chuckled. "Oh Angelica, I'm sure I'd like anything you write. You are very smart, and I want to know more about what goes on in that magnificent brain of yours."

I felts sparks running through me as her hand lightly grazed mine, as she held onto my paper. She walked away from me as her heels sounded on the floor.

Minutes passed by, and, before I knew it, class had reached its end. I sighed, realizing that meant Katherine and I would have to part ways again.

As I packed my bag however, an unexpected figure approached me. My eyes widened as I saw who it was.

"Hi Angelica." Jack greeted. This was the first time he had spoken to me this year.

He would wave at me in the hallways sometimes, but never did he speak. Not until that moment.

"Jack." I confirmed, my eyes saying it all. It was definitely a surprise. I wondered why he decided to now talk to me.

Ms. Hale marked the papers at her desk, intently reading them.

I then focused my attention back on the football player. "How may I help you?" I smiled.

"Aha. How may you help me? Hmm let's see." He placed his finger on his chin, acting as if he was thinking over it. I laughed at that, which triggered him to do so as well.

I then noticed, in the corner of my eye, a small grin on Katherine's beautiful face. She liked how I was actually engaging in someone at school.

"Um... Angelica..." He seemed nervous, losing his confidence a bit, but he still had his undeniable charm.

"Yes?" I smiled, waiting for his response.

"Prom is coming up."

"It is." I confirmed. I felt the environment in the room change. I couldn't explain it- what I meant by it- but something changed in there.

He looked into my eyes with his glistening ones as the sun rays hit them through the window. "And I was wondering if you would accompany me?" He had hoped.

My eyes widened as his unexpected words flowed through my mind. He, Jack Caprel, the most famous guy in school, wanted me to be his date to prom? But why me?

Ms. Hale held her pen tightly, with an expression on her face that was unfamiliar to me. Was she possibly... jealous? She should be happy for me.

Jack looked at me with his eyes filled with both curiosity and hope. I opened my mouth, about to say something, but a voice cut me off.

"Guys. Class is over, and I need to get going." Ms. Hale informed us, with a bit of irritation in her voice.

I bowed my head down, a bit embarrassed.

Jack then looked at me and seemed like he was mentally debating on something in his head. But then, as he became more sure of himself, he grabbed my hand, kind of forcefully, but not too rough. I looked at my hand, which was now being held inside of his. I should have felt something about it. Something magical. I mean, he was the coolest person in school, yet holding hands with him didn't bring any of those feelings to me. It wasn't the same as Katherine's.

I mentally scolded myself for thinking such a thing. After all, she was only my teacher, and she was just being friendly.

"Come with me. I'll take you home, Angel." Jack grinned.

Jack led me out of the door, still holding onto my hand, and I couldn't help but look back at Ms. Hale, who just stood frozen at her door, watching me being taken away.

I wondered how she was feeling and why she didn't stop him.

CHAPTER 5

Hours in the future

Soon I sank into deep thought, or more accurate speaking, into a complete blankness of the mind.

Katherine was like a mermaid from the bottom of the ocean, a diamond down in the depths of a cave; a lost angel.

Oh how I lost her...

Present

It was now Friday, and I walked into my last period class, feeling a bit strange. Two days ago, Jack asked me to be his date to Prom, and I never gave him an answer. I told him I would decide on Monday, but I was still not sure at all, which was crazy, because anyone in the whole world would have said yes to him instantly, without second guessing.

But, that was not my main concern. Katherine barely spoke a word to me yesterday, which yes, it was only one day, but I couldn't stand a whole day without her asking me how my day was, inviting me to her apartment, or without hearing her laugh... and her smile. I couldn't stand being away from her for so long. Physically, yes, she was always near, but mentally, she checked out, and I wanted so much for her to check back in.

Though it defied everything in me, though mentally my mind screamed it was not okay, my heart confirmed something in me at that moment.

I... I think I love her. I think I love Ms. Hale.

I loved her against reason, against hope, against everything in me that told me it was wrong.

However, I couldn't bring myself to ignore it anymore. I couldn't ignore how I felt no matter how foreign it was to me. Now, I know it to be true.

She stole my heart.

I walked into the classroom smiling as I walked past Ms. Hale. She returned the smile, grateful that I was looking at her, indifferent from yesterday.

When the bell rang, Ms. Hale began reading Hamlet to us as we took notes.

An hour had passed and another bell rang, signaling class had reached an end. I slipped my notes into my folder, which I then placed into my book bag. I then stood up, heading towards the door, before someone stopped me.

I felt a warm hand on my shoulder, causing me to halt.

"Angelica," I heard Ms. Hale uttered. "Since it's now the weekend, I thought it would be nice if we went out for the day. There's this place I want to go to with you."

A smile played on her lips, as I turned to face her.

"What do you say? Shall we go?"

I smiled as my eyes squinted at how much I was smiling. Was she asking me on a date? Or, was this normal? Was it normal for a teacher to ask a student to go somewhere with her?

Normal or not, that made my day, and there was no way I was going to decline her offer.

"Yes!" I hollered out of joy.

My cheeks immediately reddened as I felt embarrassed of showing so much excitement.

"I mean... yes. I would like that."

Ms. Hale patted me on the head and chuckled. Oh how wonderful her laugh was. It was like music to the soul.

"I would too."

She grabbed her case and reached for my hand.

"We're going to have so much fun, Angel," she assured.

I felt my heart flutter. It was definitely going to be fun.

I waited patiently in the car, looking out the window, and stared at the passing trees. It had been forty-five minutes already, and we still hadn't reached our destination. I began to wonder how much further it would be.

"Um, Ms. Hale."

"Katherine." She corrected.

"Katherine."

I repeated, smiling; remembering that she wanted me to call her by her first name outside of school.

"Hmm?" She hummed, while concentrating her eyes on the road.

"Um. How much further? And, where exactly are you taking me?" My eyes beamed due to my excitement.

"Not too far from here..." She smiled, showing her pearly-white teeth. "...and it's a surprise, Angelica."

I pouted while I crossed my arms. "But, I really want to know. It's killing me." I insisted, using my puppy dog eyes.

She started to laugh as she took a quick glance at me and my pleading expression.

"You'll live." She mocked.

I sighed. "Okay." I lightly laughed.

Eventually, Katherine pulled up into an empty parking lot and stopped the car. I guess we were here. But, what exactly was here? I hesitantly unbuckled my seat belt as I stared at the building in front of us with a confused expression on my face. It was an elongated brown building composed of brick, but it looked a bit rusty. Moreover, there was no sign or anything hinting what the place was. How did they expect for anyone to find the building? It seemed so vacant and in the middle of nowhere. What is this place?

My door flung open, and I half-smiled, seeing that it was Katherine who opened it for me.

"Thanks." I mumbled.

I hopped out and she closed the door behind me.

"Of course." She obliged. She then followed my gaze. "Don't worry. I didn't bring you all the way up here to kidnap you." She joked, watching me carefully.

"That's exactly what a kidnapper would say!" I teased back.

"Well, I am not!"

"Prove it." I crossed my arms.

She smirked as she walked away from me and towards the driver's seat. She then returned with something in her hands. It was the package.

My eyes twinkled as I wondered what was in there and why she had decided to bring it with her.

"Remember when I had received this package a few days ago?" I nodded. "Well, this is what was inside."

She smiled as she handed me the box, allowing me to open it.

My eyes sparkled as I stared at what was inside. They were skates. She had already been planning for us to go ice skating? A smile crept its way on my face as my excitement became nostalgic.

"You took me to go ice skating with you?"

She giggled. "Yea. I thought it would be fun since it's different."

I lifted the skates out of the box and held them to my chest. My cheeks reddened. "I've always wanted to go ska ting..." I got lost in Katherine's icy-blue eyes, which already were on mine. "...but my mom never was able to bring me." A tear then struck my face. "I remember the time she actually saved up enough money to be able to bring me out with her, which we hadn't been able to do for a very long time, and being the naive kid I was, I let my sudden happiness consume me. I took her words for granted. I took her for granted." I choked as I said the word "her". "But then..." Another tear. "Then she-"

Katherine tugged me into a warm embrace, holding me tight within her arms. I allowed my arms to return her embrace, and I suddenly felt them wrapping tighter around her. Eventually, when we started to part, she turned her head to the side as she wiped my tears away. She then squinted as she smiled.

"This is supposed to be a fun day, Angelica."

I stared into her eyes, at first, in confusion, but I soon redirected my stare onto the ground as my heart frowned due to my embarrassment. Nevertheless, she continued.

"Don't be a downer."

I furrowed my eyebrows and looked at her in disbelief. Her expression seemed to soften as she took a step forward.

"What happened in the past already happened. It cannot be changed." I nodded, letting her words sink into my brain. "So dwelling over it won't help you. It will only make it hurt more."

She did have a point.

I sniffled though lifted my eyes to lock onto her light blue ones that I found myself transfixed by.

"Though I don't understand what happened exactly with your mother, I know I can safely say that you didn't cause her any grief or disappointment." She pinched my cheeks. "You are too sweet for your own good, and you deserve to live a life without feeling remorse nor sadness."

She combed a hand through my hair and tucked a loose strand behind my ear.

"Let me help you. I worry about you sometimes."

I sniffled as I then glanced at her hand. Katherine Hale was incredible. No, incredible would have been an understatement. She was extraordinary. She couldn't have been compared to anyone. I had always imagined and dreamt for someone to care for me as deeply as she did, but I never imagined for the person to be my teacher.

I soon sank into deep thought, or more accurate speaking, into a complete blankness of the mind.

Katherine was like a mermaid from the bottom of the ocean, a diamond down in the depths of a cave; a lost angel.

Oh how I lost her...

I shook my head as I began to realize that I was spacing out. Without hesitation, I grabbed her hand and intertwined my fingers with hers as we then walked towards the building.

"You know." I spoke, breaking the silence. "For the longest time, that's the one thing I was afraid of. I've always regretted anyone's concern for me." I then smiled as my grasp tightened. "But, I think I'm finally ready to let someone in... and I'm glad that it's you, Katherine."

The wind blew through our hair as the world fell silent. Something was surely changing. It was as if all the cards aligned as if, no matter what, we were destined to get to this point. My lips separated ever so slightly as I felt something. Katherine's hand... she tightened her grasp as well. Heat rose to my cheeks. She undeniably had an effect on me.

CHAPTER 6

I stared into her inviting icy-blue eyes as she held onto my hands, helping me keep balance on the ice ring.

"Do you think you can stand?" She asked.

I nodded though my hands seemed to disagree with me.

"It doesn't look like it." She noticed my shaking figure. I lightly chuckled, wanting to get rid of my discomfort.

"Well, that's before I realized the ring would be this slippery," I defended myself.

I tightened my hands around hers, and seeing that I needed her to, she did the same.

She let out a mocking laugh. "It's ice, Angel. It's going to be a little slippery."

I expelled a light giggle before closing my eyes for a brief second. Focus Angelica. You can do this. It's just skating, and if I were to fall, Ms. Hale can and will catch me. See? Nothing to worry about.

I slowly released my grip on Ms. Hale as I felt my legs getting more firm and gaining equilibrium. She watched me do this, as she kept her hands in the air and close to me, in case I were to fall.

"I think I got it now," I assured.

She nodded, still eyeing me closely. I then took my first step on the ring, scooting my skates around. Then another. And another. I was doing it! So far, so good. I was worried for what? A smile crept its way on my face, and I could see Katherine smiling behind me.

She then caught up to me. "You're a natural," she complimented.

"As if," I rejected.

She let out a small laugh as she reached for my hand. My eyes widened as our fingers intertwined, and once again, I felt the same spark I felt many times before. Every cell in me tingled at her touch, and I knew why now. At least I thought I did. But, what could I do about it? Could I even tell her? It was wrong to feel this towards her, and I knew that, so wouldn't telling her put her more at risk? I didn't want to be the source of her problems. I didn't want to burden her with my feelings, especially since I wasn't sure exactly how she felt. The more we skated, the more I felt my knees becoming weak. Probably due to exhaustion, but I knew that I could still skate for a while longer. I then glanced at my hand, which Katherine continued to hold.

"How long is she going to keep that there?" I thought. I then realized that my stare must have lasted longer than I expected, because she began to stare as well. She definitely caught me. I gulped as I turned away, which just made her giggle. I then slowly released my hand from her grasp. I didn't want to. It felt strange, as if my hand belonged there, but I knew it was beginning to be too long for the kind of relationship we had. Her eyes widened as I started to gain speed, directing myself away from her.

"Um. Are you okay?" She questioned.

Being the awesome skater she was, she managed to catch up to me quickly, yet I still tried to challenge her.

"Yea. What makes you ask that?" I panted.

"You..." She took a gasp for air. "You just... sped away from me as if I was some sort of enemy."

"Oh," was all I could manage to say. It wasn't that. She had it all wrong. It's just the contrary, but I was not going to tell her that.

"Oh?" She mocked.

"Yea," I retorted.

She then pulled my arm, catching me off guard, and before we knew it, she fell on top of me, leaving me with the recoil.

"Ugh." I winced.

Her eyes softened. "I'm sorry... I didn't mean for..." She searched for words while mine parted.

"This is why, if you must know. This is why I sped away." I closed my eyes as I turned my head to the side, still under her, encaged by her arms.

She arched a brow. "Because, you thought I would fall on you? Because, I'm that clumsy?" She laughed. "I guess I've proven to be just that." She confirmed, still laughing.

I shook my head. "No. Because... you... you just." I gulped. What was I doing? "You make me feel complete. Being around you makes me feel happier than I ever thought I could feel. And, it surprises me how fond I am of you." I bit my lip. "I never felt this before, and I don't know what to do about it but run."

My eyes then widened as I realized what just slipped out of my mouth. It surprised me. I never planned on saying anything over the matter. yet it just burst out of me. It did feel good to finally let go of my burdensome feelings, however.

I turned my face towards her and she reached out a hand, soon caressing my cheek. My brows furrowed in confusion, yet I didn't stop her. I felt the electricity flowing from her hand to my cheek like a completed circuit. I couldn't help but grin, submissively.

"Angelica..."

Her lips curved into a smile as she softly spoke my name. I felt her hot breath over me, which sent chills throughout my body.

"I'm not running."

My lips parted due to shock. I didn't expect her response to be that. She then continued.

"And, you don't have to feel the need to run from me. What you're feeling right now, that joy and excitement that occupies your heart right now."

She placed her hand on my chest, where my heart would be.

"It's because you care about me." Her grin widened. "And, that feeling cannot be inflicted without another."

She stared intently into my deep-ocean eyes as I stared into her icy-blue ones. My heart thudded harshly against my chest, and I knew she could feel my pulse through her hand.

"You know, the day we met, I failed you beyond measure."

My brows arched as I continued to pierce her eyes with my intense stare. What did she mean she "failed me beyond measure?"

Swallowing, her eyes downturned. "The moment I took your hand and you looked at me, with the glory of hate in your eyes. I should have sent you home to your dad. But, I didn't. I didn't want to."

"No, no. I never hated you." I clarified.

I didn't want her to get the wrong idea. When did I ever say that I hated her?

"Aha, but a part of you did. Your heart did, and it's okay."

She bit her lip as her light eyes sweetly glanced upon me.

"There was honesty in your hatred. Fearlessness in your pain. And, in that honesty, I saw a reflection of myself. I then began to realize, I dreaded the moments when our hands released; I dreaded the moments when our stares broke. I didn't want to let you go." She confessed.

"Then don't," I suggested.

I didn't know what it was exactly. I didn't know what had possessed me in that moment, but my body ached to be closer to hers. Feeding off of that urge, I cupped her face in my hands and leaned in half way, breaking the once space between us. She leaned in as well, and I could feel her pulse against my chest at this point. Awe, her pulse was as rapid as mine. A smile soon crept on my lips as they had lightly brushed Katherine's. Our lips moved rhythmically with each other's, growing more and more intense, but never once did one of our tongues slip into the other's mouth. The kiss was calm and a little hesitant, but it was definitely a sweet kiss. A more polite one.

A few seconds later, I slowly opened my eyes, my lips still locked on hers, and I noticed a tear running down her face. Why was she crying? It hurt me to see her cry. It always pained my heart. It made me feel guilty though I knew it was not my fault. Deep down, I felt like it was though. I broke the kiss before it could become too heavy because I knew we were not ready for that kind of kiss yet.

I caressed her cheeks as she did to mine before. I then wiped away her tear and kissed where it once was. This made her smile as she sniffled.

"Why were you crying?" I dared to ask. "Did you not like the kiss?" I knew that she did. There was no way that could have been one-sided, but I needed her to tell me why she was feeling pain at that moment. A kiss was meant to leave a mark of happiness and admiration. Was it not?

"No." She muttered, defeated. "It's just that I feel very fortunate to have met you." She smiled, earnestly.

I smiled back as I giggled.

"I feel the same." I admitted.

A thought then came to my attention, and so I quickly but carefully leaned forward, causing Katherine to stand up. She held out her hand, which I took. I balanced myself up and stood.

"Katherine," I spoke her name with excitement.

"Yes?" She questioned. There was curiosity now in her eyes.

"Let's take a picture together." I squealed. "I never want to forget this moment."

There was a look in her eyes. A look that I couldn't really read, but she nodded, assuring me that it was fine.

I excitedly skated towards my bag, which had my phone in it, and I skated my way back towards Katherine.

"Don't forget to smile." I joked as I held the phone out in front of us.

Snap. I looked at the photo of the two of us together. Our cheeks brushed against each other's as our smiles didn't look forced at all. It looked genuine and real.

"Now I will never forget the day I skated with my teacher." I teased.

She laughed along with me. "You better." She mocked, gaining her fun spirit back. "Hey." She then grabbed my hand and led me off of the ring by her side. "It's only seven p.m., but do you have any place where you have to be right now?" I shook my head. "Good, because there's one more place I want to go with you before I let you go."

I frowned. "I can't stay at your house tonight?"

"It would probably be best if you stayed at your house for a while. I don't want your dad to grow suspicious of your whereabouts." She had a point.

"Okay." I sighed, but a smile quickly crossed my face as I wondered where she would be taking me.

The day had already been probably the best day of my life. Being with her made me feel amazing and so complete. Moreover, I've always wanted to go skating, and I got to go with Katherine.

"Where are you taking me?" I asked, excitement filling my eyes,

She held her index finger to her lips. "Shhh. It's a surprise, Angelica." She smiled. "You'll love it."

"Impossible."

"Huh?"

"Love is a strong word, Ms. Hale."

She arched a brow as a hidden smirk rested on her lips.

"I can't love more than one thing. I can only like wherever you're taking me. Just like I only like skating." I clarified.

"What is it you love then? Since there can only be one?" She asked, playfully.

I looked intently into her eyes.

"Well isn't it obvious."

CHAPTER 7

K atherine Hale's P.O.V.

I stared into the dark of the night and got lost in the stars. How beautiful and transcended it looked up there. I had always admired the sky and the mysterious things that occurred beyond our world. Beyond Earth.

"I can see why you brought me here," I heard Angelica's soft voice beside me. "It's so beautiful and peaceful here... and I love the vastness of the sky."

I smiled. "I used to go here all of the time to clear my thoughts."

We were on top of this grassy hill where we could practically look down at the city. And, being up so high made me feel more close and more drawn to the stars.

"Out of curiosity, what about the sky intrigues you?" I wondered what answer she would give me.

"Hmm..." She wore a thoughtful expression on her face as she pondered what it was, herself. A smile quickly appeared on her face. "I don't know exactly why, but when I look at the sky, I feel as if I'm at home. I feel... comfort and peace watching the stars above me."

My eyes widened. Looking at the sky seemed to induce the same effect on her as to me.

The look in her eyes then changed. They began to sparkle as she pierced her eyes into mine.

"I feel the same when I'm with you," she realized.

My lips separated ever so slightly as her words pounded in my mind. She felt safe with me, and that's all I had ever wanted her to feel. Ever since I saw her face, and those beautiful ocean-like eyes, filled with fear, I made it my mission to protect her. It made my heart frown that such an angel, such a gift from God, was being tormented and abused.

It wasn't right.

No one should have that much pain in their life. Especially not her.

Yet, she had gone around still believing in the good in the world... and in all of the people. She genuinely believed that.

She didn't see the bad. Or merely, she did a great job ignoring it.

I pursed my lips as I shifted my body again, facing the sky. If only you knew... how much you mean to me, Angelica. If only...

"Angelica," I breathed.

Her head was still facing mine, so I knew she was completely tuned in to what I was about to say next. I gave her an assuring smile as I reached for her hand.

"I know I'm your teacher, and you probably only think of me as your teacher." I got lost in her eyes. "But-"

My words were interrupted with another kiss from Angelica. My eyes widened but soon softened as I scooted closer to her, wrapping my arms around her waist. Her hands found their way around my neck as she began trailing kisses down my cheek and nibbling on my ear. I felt her hot breath on my neck, causing my nerves to run wild. I couldn't believe how this girl made me feel. She was worth my time. She was worth me coming back for her every time.

My eyes awakened as I slowly and gently pushed her away from me, but never once letting go of her arms. I just left my hands there, not able to move them.

I noticed the look in her eyes changing again. She looked as if she were lost. She didn't know what we were doing. She didn't know what this was, but it was clear that whatever it was... it was real. More real than anything else in the world. And, no matter how hard I tried to reject these feelings, my heart would always remind me that they were there.

I didn't think I could ever lose those feelings, and I never did.

Angelica Rose's P.O.V.

I felt her warm skin as I pressed my lips onto her cheek. A part of me was hesitant still, though every kiss made my heart pound louder and louder for her. And, each kiss I planted on her smooth face reconfirmed my infatuation. Just as I hovered my lips over her chin, I felt hands lightly pushing me away, yet they never left my arms, as if warning me that we should stop, though she didn't want me to. I looked, calculatingly, at her baffled expression, trying to figure out what she was thinking, but I couldn't read her. I was always so good at reading people, but with her, it was different. It was as if she had built up a wall, a facade, blocking me from knowing everything that ran through her mind, in order to protect herself.

I then thought about what she had just said. I did this twice now. She would confess on touchy subjects that would put a strain on her heart, yet instead of giving her a proper reply, I would shush her with a kiss. In a way, though, a kiss could speak a lot on its own. It basically told her that I understood how she was feeling. But, I knew I should say something, rather than just assume she knew. With that resolve, I cleared my throat and spoke up.

"I don't understand this. It confuses me." I pointed my finger at Katherine and then at me, gesturing that we were the "this". "But..." I bit my lip, and my voice seemed to soften on its own, though it had already been light to begin with. "But, you have it all wrong. I don't only think of you as my teacher. That I know for sure. I mean, we kissed!" My eyes sparkled as my heart fluttered at the recognition of being kissed by Katherine. Katherine light-heartedly smiled, which only made me feel more compelled to explain further. I placed my fingers on my lips and felt them. "That was my first kiss." I confessed.

"Really?" Katherine was in shock.

"Yea." I began to blush. "I never felt so much desire and the need to kiss anyone... until today." I admitted.

I stared into Katherine's glistening blue orbs, which after a while, seemed to grow more and more lost into the darkness. I began contemplating whether to speak more or to continue our uninvited silence. I bit my lip and shifted my eyes a bit from hers to the surrounding behind her. Was she going to ever say something? She wouldn't just let the night end here, would she?

Katherine caught my gaze again as her lips wavered. She seemed as if she were thinking over what the right response would have been, though in reality, none of this would have been considered "right". In the eyes of everyone else, we would be frowned upon if seen together like this. But, with her, it felt so surreal. It felt like we had abandoned reality and entered another realm- one where anything was possible.

"I'm glad, but it won't happen again." I felt my heart aching in my chest as I heard Katherine's shattering words.

It won't happen again?

"Like I said, I failed you beyond measure. When I look at you, I see a reflection of myself... or who I want to be." She sighed. "But, I am your teacher."

I concentrated my eyes on the sky above me. I thought it would be less painful channeling all of my attention on the vacant space above me rather than the conversation that left me feeling confused... and possibly... mislead?

"You're my teacher." I restated, really to confirm this to myself.

I knew she was, yet my mind seemed not to grasp the severity of it all. There were many consequences for what we were doing.

"And?" I challenged.

"And?" She mimicked.

"So what if you are my teacher. You said it before, yourself." She arched a brow, and so I clarified. "I remember the night we watched Princess Bride, and I remember our talk. You told me that if you love someone so much, it's worth the risk. So... am I not worth the risk for you?"

I bit my lip, a flash of hope concealed within my eyes.

"I already told you how I feel. I mean, I'm so confused as it is, being I've never experienced anything like this, but you can help me. Help me understand." I pleaded.

I grabbed her hands and cupped them with mine, which surprised both of us.

"Be my teacher."

Silence filled our surroundings before Katherine soon broke it.

"You're right." Katherine acknowledged. I am? "I did say that, didn't I?" She lightly chuckled.

"Did you mean it? Or was it just your professional literature-self talking?" I mentally slapped myself. How could I joke at a time like this?

"No." I felt the pain in my chest lift at her one word response. "I meant what I said. I do believe it is worth it, when you find the one person you can't live without- when you find the one person that makes you feel more complete than when you are without her."

You complete me. That phrase resonated with me somehow. Her lips curved into a smile as she pecked my lips.

"I can't live without you in my life, Angelica. There is no denying that. But, for now, for both of our sakes, it would be best if we were only friends outside of school."

My lips curved into a frown.

"So, it really was our final kiss."

I hated thinking I wouldn't be able to kiss her again, at least for a while.

She giggled, which made my heart float in my chest.

"We have a long time ahead of us." She then gave me a wink as she said the words, "Who can say for certain?"

The wind howled, sending shivers down both of our spines. A sudden storm was brewing in the sky as if disagreeing with what we were talking about. I guess even nature didn't want us to "only be friends". Nature was on our side.

So I had thought.

"Looks like there will be a storm tonight. What a shame." She helped me up, after standing up, herself. She seemed unfazed, however.

"Yea." I sighed.

I didn't know when I would ever hang out with Katherine like this, after our talk that finalized our friendship and nothing more. I didn't want the night to end. Why did the storm have to interrupt us?

After a long while in Katherine's car, we finally reached her house. She stopped the engine, popped an umbrella open and rushed out of her door in order to open mine.

She was always so polite. One of her many qualities.

I lied on Katherine's couch with a heater next to me because it was becoming chilly outside, and I covered my body in one of the cozy blankets she gave me. Though she told me it wouldn't happen, she allowed me to sleep at her house once again tonight. I was starting to get used to being here.

"Good night. Sweet Dreams, Angelica." I heard Katherine's sweet tender voice from a few feet away.

Her room happened to be adjacent from the living room, so I could hear and see her as she called out, standing by her bedroom door.

"They'll only be sweet if you're in them." I teased, flirtatiously. Seriously, what has gotten into me?

An approving giggle sounded in my ears before I closed my eyes, allowing for my thoughts to drift off to another place...

CHAPTER 8

Angelica's P.O.V.

A merciless hand rose, seeking blood. It wanted to cause pain in me, but it was no different from any other circumstance. This time, however, he lost all control. All of the humanity within him seemed nonexistent as his devilish grin grew after my every dropping tear. My crying seemed to fuel his happiness.

"You good for nothing daughter!" He yelled as he slapped my face. "You are the reason your mother isn't here."

"N-No..." I cried. "You said she crashed in a car accident. Dad, did you forget what you told me?"

I searched his expression, which seemed both frazzled and hopeless. Yet, he still believed I had killed her.

"I lied." He scowled. "I wanted to protect you because I knew how much you looked up to her. But..." His voice lowered as he continued with, "you are the reason for her death. You were always so weak and depended way too much on the woman. You overworked her, and she died from all of the stress."

His eyes sent daggers through mine with his intense stare.

"She died, worrying too much about you." He made clear.

"N-no." I stuttered in disbelief. "I did not kill my mother."

Was it possible that I did? Was there truth in what my dad was saying? If I find out that I did, I couldn't live with myself.

"I-I didn't." I repeated, though more shakily.

"Own up to your sins right now! God can't forgive you when all you're able to do is lie." I wasn't lying. At least, I don't think I am?

I covered my face with my hands as Daddy stomped his way closer and closer to me. No no no. This couldn't be happening. I didn't kill her. Please... someone tell me I was not the reason for her death.

I felt cold hands grabbing at mine.

"Please don't! I'm sorry!" I cried.

The hands rubbed gently on mine, in a nourishing way. Confused at this sudden change, I poked my head out of my hands and looked at the presence in front of me.

Instead of being in the living room with my dad, my body was transported to the distant meadows with none other than Katherine. My hands trembled underneath hers as my mind remained lost in the darkness that my dad stirred inside of me.

The woman looked at me with her warming, light eyes.

"I can help you."

My eyes widened. "But, this is a dream. You aren't real." A tear struck my face at the realization that Katherine wasn't really by my side, comforting me. "You can't help me."

Katherine's expression softened as her eyes remained locked onto mine. "A dream is an experience, and an experience is real." She spoke. "Do you understand?"

My eyes watered as I nodded. "I think so."

She wiped the tears from my eyes, though hers were evidently beginning. "Don't cry." She obliged. "You're stronger than this."

"In what way am I strong?" I sniffled in despair. "I can't defend myself against my dad, I can't stop the bullying, I let my mom die." My sniffling worsened. "And, for all of this time, I was waiting for someone like you... but now you're slowly slipping away."

I cried in Katherine's open arms as she tightened them. I was a mess. Still holding me close to her body, she spoke somewhat in a whisper.

"You don't believe any of that, do you?"

I felt a tear falling from her cheek and onto my shoulder. She didn't have any strength left to restrain from crying.

"Angelica," she squealed. "All of the bad events that sur-round your life do not determine the amount of strength you possess. No one in the world understands what you're going through, and if you ask me, it would be hard for you to deal with it any better than you already have." She pressed her lips on my cheek, sending a warming feeling through my skin and towards my heart. "And, I am not slipping away. You see? I'm here."

I shook my head. "If you're here, then why do I feel as though you're fading away?"

"Angelica, I-"

I panted as my eyes awakened from my slumber. What a terrible nightmare. I felt tears running down my face. It felt as if it were real, though I knew it was only a dream.

In that moment, I realized something, however. I didn't want to be weak anymore.

Though I couldn't prevent my mom's death, or any of my problems from starting, maybe I could finally end them.

I tiptoed my way downstairs and, through the crack of the door, saw that my dad was still asleep. I got to the kitchen and quickly popped a piece of bread in the toaster oven, and I grabbed a glass of orange juice. I never wanted to make too much noise in the mornings, so I never made anything more, though I probably should have at least cooked some eggs for the protein factor.

Nevertheless, I was off to school.

I walked down the hallway towards seventh period until a familiar presence greeted me.

"Hey, Angelica. Wait up!"

Jack stopped me in my tracks as he panted with his hands on his knees.

"Good afternoon." I smiled, sweetly.

"Good afternoon." He repeated.

He straightened his spine, prior to returning my smile.

"So, did you decide yet? About prom?"

Oh right. It was Monday now, and I needed to make a decision. In all honesty, the main reason I didn't have an answer for him was because of my feelings for Katherine, but after Friday, after she told me that we could only be friends, I guess I could go with Jack. There was no longer an issue.

"Right." I scratched my head. "Yea. I think it would be a lot of fun. Thanks for inviting me. It's an honor that you want me to accompany you." I smiled from ear to ear. I mean, he was the star quarterback. I was still surprised he wanted to go with me and not one of the cheerleaders.

"No." He expelled a half-chuckle. "I am the one who is honored."

He grinned as his eyes trailed over me, from head to toe.

"You are gorgeous."

Gorgeous? Did he just call me gorgeous?

"Thanks."

My cheeks started to redden, and so I tried to end the conversation with the excuse that we needed to get to class.

He nodded while he wore a minuscule smile before he slipped his hand into mine, and we walked in. I didn't reject his hand, though there was no spark or anything electrifying by his touch.

Not everyone was in their seats yet, but it seemed as if Jack and I were close to the last ones to come in, which made me feel nauseous. I was usually always there early.

"I'll talk to you after class," he whispered into my ear as his hand started uncurling from mine.

I nodded as I made my way to my seat.

Everyone started to stare at me, and I figured it was because I came in with the most popular kid in school and with my hand glued to his.

I noticed him smiling towards me as he sat in his usual seat a couple of seats away from mine. I gave him a cheeky smile back as I grabbed my folder out of my bag. I wondered what we were about to learn.

Ms. Hale swiftly got up, from behind her desk, and made her way to the front. Our eyes met for a brief second before she quickly turned away and focused on the whole class as a whole. I knew she asked for me to be her friend, but at the rate this was going, it seemed as if she was terrified of the idea alone. It made me wonder...

It was as if she didn't want to get too close to me, though she failed, considering I practically depended on her and her support. I never told her that merely because I didn't want her to think I was too needy or clingy. The last thing I wanted was to give her more of a reason to stay clear of me.

"I've finally gotten to your papers from last week."

Ms. Hale spoke while grabbing a tray filled with our essays.

"And, you guys have done well. It would be kind of hard to fail an assignment that was open to many and all possibilities." She jested.

My eyes widened as she walked over to my desk and handed me half of the papers.

"Would you mind helping me pass these out, Ms. Rose?" She gave me a warm smile, and I nodded, accepting the work.

I watched in awe as she walked away from me in her clanking heels.

"Looking Sexy." Cameron winked at me as I handed his essay.

I just smiled as I continued on. The outfit I was wearing also happened to come from Ms. Hale's closet. She told me to wear it today, and so I did. I wore a black ruffled blouse and blue jeans with a belt. I've got to admit. She had a great sense of style- something I lacked. But, being around her allowed me to catch on.

A boy licked his lips as he stared at my hand, which was extending for him to receive his paper.

"Are you going to just leave me here with your essay? Or are you going to take it?" I teased, playfully.

It was unlike me to be so confident and forward around anyone- anyone but Katherine- but I had convinced myself that I would try to change in order to stop all of my problems. My shyness had to go...

"Uh..." He continued to stare at my hand, and then directed his eyes on me. "Yea." He decided, with nervousness in his voice.

The people around him smirked as they watched the boy become anxious around me- the once known little shy Christian girl. Nathaniel raised a brow as he grabbed his paper out of my hand, when I got to his desk.

"Making fun of Kyle, are you? It's not his fault that you suddenly became attractive. You can't blame him for being confused." A smirk was plastered on his face. "And, it's been more than one day. Has it been a week?" He turned to one of his buddies. "Aha. Who is she trying to impress?" His buddy shrugged in response.

I cleared my throat as I pondered on what my reaction should have been.

"Only myself." I smiled, which only made Nathaniel's forehead crease in confusion.

"And me!" Jack chimed in, with a cheeky grin. "Looking hot, babe." He winked as he stood up, making his presence known.

Ms. Hale watched us with a disturbed look in her eyes. Was it anger? Disappointment maybe?

"Enough talking, class." She silenced us.

I bit my lip as I noticed her eyes focusing on me, yet I pretended not to notice.

Eventually, I finished passing out all of them, and so I sat back down in my seat. Noticing my essay, I grabbed it firmly in my hands. I got an "A" plus, which was amazing, but that was not the only thing that caught my eye. There was a sticky note also. I tore it off, careful not to rip it, and then I read it.

Angelica,

I didn't mean to pry, but I guess I'm a bit curious. When you wrote this, why did you decide on talking about your dreams? Nevertheless, it was well written, but I'm worried why it is you get continuous dreams of the meadows. And, are the people in your dreams people you know in real life? It could be confusing if your dreams parallel a lot of reality.

I'm not a physiologist, but you should probably think about your dreams a bit more. Your mind sometimes knows more than you can remember.

-Ms. Hale

I placed the sticky note back where it was on my essay, and I tilted my head up. Katherine's eyes were already on me, watching me do this. I forgot what I wrote about. I forgot that I wrote about my continuous dreams of the Meadows, but I never told her that she was in them. That wouldn't have been appropriate.

We read some more of Hamlet, and soon the bell rang, dismissing us. And, let me tell you, the more days that had passed, the more I dreaded the moments when the bell would ring. I just didn't want to go home.

"Hey." Katherine spoke to me as everyone was slowly dispersing.

"Hi." I responded as I began packing my bag.

"How are you?" She unconsciously bit her lip as she waited for my response.

My bottom lip slightly separated from the top, but Jack snuck from behind me and yelled, "Boo!"

I felt my heart pounding in my chest at the sudden movement and sound. I playfully slapped his arm in response.

Ms. Hale began walking away from me and back towards her desk. I stared at her moving feet and then at her evident expression on her face as she reached for her case.

"We discussed that we would talk after class, remember? So let's talk!" Jack recalled, paying no attention to Ms. Hale's bothered expression.

Taking note of it, however, I grabbed his hand and led him out of the classroom with me.

"We did?" I arched a brow as a curious smirk played on my face. "What did you want to talk about?" I asked.

"Um." He scratched his head as he went into deep thought. "I want to know the color of the dress you will be wearing so that I can get a matching tie and, of course, the corsage."

I stared past Jack, but rather, at the wall behind him. I didn't think that far ahead, though I probably should have, considering prom was literally the Friday of that week.

"Green." Katherine answered for me as she walked out. Huh?

I arched a brow, perplexed, as I waited for her to clarify.

She smiled. "I've had this green dress just locked in my closet for a while having no use. I've been meaning to give it away." She took a breath before allowing a smile to cross her face, showing her laugh lines. "Why don't you wear it for this special occasion?" She insisted.

She would really give me her dress, basically marking her approval of me going with Jack to prom? This made me feel strange. I felt a bit relieved that I had her blessing, but I couldn't help but also feel a little torn that she didn't seem to mind me going with him rather than her. Though of course, we both knew I couldn't go with her anyway.

"Thanks, Ms. Hale." I took her offer, though I had remained in my self-inflicted battle on what it all meant.

"Wow." Jack was starstruck. "Ms. Hale is like the best teacher. I wish I had a male teacher who would just lend me his tux whenever." He chuckled at his own comment before waving me off.

I laughed as I waved back. Jack was different from everyone's expectations. He was not the typical macho football player who was self-centered, vain and rude. He was sweet, and he had a sense of humor.

Katherine laid a hand over my shoulder, which caused me to jump a little. Her touch gave me reminiscence of my dream. She smiled as she watched my cheeks redden due to my embarrassment.

"It would be my pleasure."

"Um... what?"

She smirked. "To lend you my dress," she clarified.

"Right." I squinted as my nerves got the best of me.

"I'll give you a ride home, okay? And, on the way, we'll stop by my place, and I'll show you the dress." She patted my head as if I was her dependent puppy.

I nodded. "I bet it's as beautiful as you," I stupidly remarked.

I mentally face palmed at my childish comment.

She let out a light chuckle, and a few seconds later, planted her lips on my cheek, sending an electrifying kind of warmth throughout my body.

My eyes, which were once widened, soon softened as I savored her unexpected affection.

Her lips curved into a smile as her lips distanced itself from my cheek, making it miss the connection. "Beauty isn't about having a pretty face. It's about having a pretty mind, a pretty heart, and most importantly, a beautiful soul." Katherine's eyes seemed dilated as it saw right through me. "No one can compare to your beauty."

I shook my head. How could she say all of those pretty words to me and say I'm beautiful when she barely knew who I was. She's only been my teacher for barely over a week. I pressed my fingers against my blouse, right over my stomach, as I remembered the scars that hid beneath. I slowly lifted my shirt over my head, exposing my skin in front of my teacher.

"I'm not pretty," I denied, feeling ashamed of my flawed body. "I have so many imperfections."

My chin lowered, yet Katherine used her finger to hold my chin up as honesty continued to fill her eyes.

"There is a kind of beauty in imperfection." Katherine convinced me.

I tilted my head to the side as I glanced upon her beautiful face and her amazing figure. She had the lightest blue eyes, that you would fall for every time they stared in your direction, dirty blond wavy hair, that was like a sunset, becoming lighter at the tips, and she had flawless skin.

"How could something like this happen?" I thought to myself. I was sent a gift. The most perfect gift.

Katherine Hale couldn't have been more perfect, and I felt more than fortunate that she allowed me to get to know her and that she took interest in me.

"But..." seriousness and severity unfolded in her eyes. "I won't let any of that happen to you again, Angelica. I knew you had scars, but I didn't know there were this many." Her eyes frowned as she glared at every one of them. "I can help you."

"You can't help me." I shook my head. "You aren't with me all of the time." I then began to mumble as I said, "you aren't with me when I'm at home."

She seemed to hear me because she then responded with "Then let's change that."

My eyes widened as I stared into her earnest eyes. Did I hear her right? Was she really planning on being with me twenty-four/seven in order to prevent my beatings?

"Why would you though?" I cleared my throat. "Why would you do all of these things for me? A student you barely know?"

She breathed out as she considered her answer. Her smile then widened as she gave me a vague response.

"One day, you'll understand why." I looked at her, dumbfounded. She then continued with, "Just think of me as your guardian angel... I will protect you... even if it hurts me in the end."

Even if it hurts me in the end. Those words, in particular, resonated through my mind for a while.

CHAPTER 9

I neatly hung the green dress in my closet and then jumped into a lying position on my bed. I started thinking about what Ms. Hale had told me on the sticky note. Maybe she was right. Maybe I was missing something, and my dreams were trying to give me a message that my conscious self seemed to have forgotten.

Let's see. In my last dream, my dad practically blamed me for my mother's death, and, for some reason, I was vulnerable and had believed it to be a possibility. I knew I did not cause her death. She had never shown any signs that I was stressing her out. In fact, she complimented my easiness and for always following her directions and rules. I didn't give her any problems.

So, what was I missing? How come my mind felt the need to put me in such a strange place?

And, just when my mind felt like exploding from the torturing thoughts of my mother's death and my dad accusing,

Katherine sent an angelic touch my way in which saved me and gave me comfort. She managed to be my guardian angel even in my dreams.

I smiled as I thought about her essence and how she made me feel so at ease when she was near. There was something about her that would always make my heart flutter with excitement. I then remembered the pictures we took the night we went out together, and I was intrigued to look back at them, I rushed out of my bed and towards the handbag that I had them in. I felt the photos in between my fingers as I studied them.

"We looked so happy there," I thought to myself.

I looked at my face and the genuine and wide grin contained in my expression as my arm held her close to me. I then stared at Katherine's face. I didn't realize it then, but now, Katherine's face revealed something different. Her expression... yes she was smiling... but sometimes a smile could be misleading and hiding the truth. I creased my forehead and squinted my eyes as I continued to focus on her mysterious expression. What was she thinking? How was she feeling? I was in such a great mood, and so, I guess I just assumed she would reciprocate those feelings. But, this photo recognized something I couldn't.

Sadness.

"I don't want to forget this moment," I remembered telling her.

And, ever since, or maybe prior to that, she had felt gloomy. Did she think I wouldn't remember? It was as if she knew that taking a picture wouldn't help me remember. Absurd, wasn't it?

I chuckled lightly to myself at the idea. If that was the reason, she worried too much. See where worrying gets you? It makes you think all sorts of weird outcomes that most likely wouldn't happen.

I then thought back on what she told me the first time I came to her house, right before she lost it.

"Angelica..."

I tilted my head up, locking my eyes on hers as I anticipated on her next words.

"Do you know why I called you here? Do you remember me saying why?"

She seemed as if she wanted me, with all of her heart, to say that I did. But, she was confused. She never said anything.

"You never told me..." I uttered, getting lost in her blue eyes.

"Hmm..."

She looked away for a second, and I could tell she was struggling with something in her head. It was hurting me to see her like this, and it killed me not knowing why.

"Ugh!" I heard her almost yell. Though I knew that her sudden outburst was clearly directed at herself, it shocked me, and so, involuntarily, I jumped off of the couch.

I watched as Ms. Hale knocked over her lamp, a few stacks of paper and a few plates- the sound of the glass shattering sounding an alarm in my ears.

I cried out in pain. Not a physical pain, but an emotional one.

I was so wrong about her.

This whole time she made me feel so happy and safe, but here she was, destroying her own apartment over a confusion.

I was watching my teacher completely lose it.

I slowly backed away from her, my heart racing uncontrollably in my chest.

But then, something changed... her eyes... they seemed to change- like she had just seen a phantom.

Ms. Hale dropped the paper that was once in her hand, and then, I saw a tear sneak its way down her cheek as realization struck her.

She frantically turned around and walked towards me, but I backed up slowly at every step she took.

"Angelica... I'm so sorry..." she cried.

My eyes started to water, matching hers. I didn't know what to say or how to feel.

"I shouldn't have pressured you to remember something that you clearly did not... I mean, I knew you didn't. There was no way, yet I completely freaked out on you."

She tried grabbing my arm, but she missed as I stepped back out of fear.

"You never told me anything."

Even then, she had that fear... that I would somehow forget something... something important.

I got out from my sitting position, with the pictures in hand, and opened the first drawer of my dresser. There lied an empty notebook, and so, I grabbed it and opened it to the first page. I had decided that this would be the perfect place to keep all of my new photos.

I then closed the book and placed it back in the drawer when a noise sounded from downstairs.

I felt my heart beating rapidly in my chest as the sudden commotion startled me.

"Dance with me!" Dad.

I poked my head out of my door and got a glimpse of his appearance as he walked drunken-like in the kitchen. It was the middle of the day. I wondered what had happened to make him want to numb the senses.

"I said dance with me, Clarise."

He started dancing around with his hands out as if some-one were beside him, but no one was. My eyes widened at the name "Clarise". He was imagining a confrontation with my mother.

I gulped as I crept my way downstairs, debating whether I should go to him- to my father. I shook my head and let out a sigh as I persuaded my feet to continue on.

"Mom is not here right now," I asserted, noticing my dad's spine stiffening as my presence seemed to have star- tled him.

He turned around slowly as a tear fought its way out of his eyes. It was rare to seem him in this state, so it caught me off guard. His bottom lip began separating from the top, and then, it began to shake as his nerves went haywire.

"When will she be back?"

His question made my heart ache. It was happening again. He would get very drunk, and then, he would ask me where his dead wife was, and what was I supposed to say?

I gulped once more as I placed my hand on his shoulder.

"She c-can't come back."

I lowered my eyes to the floor as I felt my own tears fighting their way out. I then took a deep breath as I tried to stay strong, for his sake.

"But, we will see her again."

"When?"

His voice was shaky, and I saw the look of desperation in his eyes, mixed with a glimpse of hope.

I half-heartedly chuckled in disbelief as I wiped a tear that dared to sneak its way down my face.

"I-I don't know."

He looked around, seeming lost.

"But, I want to see her."

His voice was soft enough to be carried through the air.

He leaned in to take another sip of the Vodka that was in his hands when I quickly, but carefully, took it out of his grasp.

"I don't think you need any more of this right now." I acknowledged.

He nodded before piercing my eyes with his. Something was connecting within him as he looked at me differently than before.

"I'm so sorry," he vocalized. "I'm so sorry for hurting you. You told me that I was taking too much, that alcohol was beginning to control me and my life, yet-" He sniffled as his eyes watered more. "Yet I took another sip!"

I arched my brow in confusion. He then inched forward and pulled me into his arms. I returned his embrace. I felt sorry my mom's absence had such a toll on him.

"I didn't mean to hurt you, Clarise." Ah, I see. He thought I was my mother. "But, know this. It wasn't me who was hurting you, for I wouldn't ever! It was the alcohol."

"What do you mean? What did you do to her?"

I stepped back from his embrace as both rage and sadness seeped through my eyes.

"I-I..." He dropped to his knees, holding his face in his hands. "I killed her... the accident was a cover up because the truth was too hard to admit."

My hands, which were now dropped to my sides, clenched into fists as his words echoed in my mind.

"You what?"

"I-I killed your mother!" He screamed.

He was so lost in his self-pity to even notice he had admitted his crime to his one and only daughter.

"I can't believe you! You ruined our family!"

I ran towards the bottle of Vodka that was lying on the counter. I grasped the bottle in my hand and threw it onto the ground. The sound of shattering glass filled the small kitchen, bouncing off of the white walls. Normally, I would wince at such a startling noise, but I was too overwhelmed by my emotions to care at the time.

"Was it worth it?" I squealed. "This freakin' alcohol? Was it worth sacrificing my mother?"

I felt my heart thudding beneath my chest, and all I could think about, in that moment, was that I wanted to silence it; I wanted to silence the pain and the heartache.

He crawled to my feet and held onto one of my legs, pleading for my forgiveness.

"I promise you, I-I will get help." He sniffled. "I want to rebuild this family. I can fix it."

"Pfft. You can't fix anything! She's already gone. You can't bring her back from the grave!"

I shook my leg loose and ran towards my room to get my bag.

"Where are you going?" He questioned, limply following me.

"Anywhere but here!" I yelled from upstairs as I began packing.

I then ran downstairs towards the front door, losing my breath.

All of this time, he, my father, was responsible for my beloved mother's death. There were no words that could possibly describe how I was feeling at that moment. It was more than just detest, more than hatred, more than remorse; more than betrayal. There needed to be a word that could sum that up into one meaning. I needed that word.

I felt the doorknob within my hand. I took a sigh before twisting it before my heart then stopped, and my eyes widened. My mind screamed that something was wrong. No, everything was wrong about this, but I didn't care to question it. Tears streamed down my face as I jumped into the arms of the woman in front of me.

Time seemed to stop as her words broke through me and reached my soul.

"I'm sorry I've been gone for a while, Sweetie." The woman spoke. "But, I'm here now, and I will never leave you again."

Oh mom!

Dad lifted his head out of his hands as he glared at his long lost wife, in confusion. I think he really believed he had killed her. I couldn't even imagine how relieved and blessed he must have felt in that instant.

"Clarise..." He acknowledged as he began crawling towards us. "I don't understand." His eyes communicated his confusion.

"Some things aren't meant to be understood." Her gentle voice spoke. Her gaze then shifted to the smashed bottle on the ground before she turned her head back towards his face. "And, I see you haven't given up on alcohol yet. Have you?" There was a definite hint of disapproval and shame in her voice.

Dad frowned as he nodded.

"But, I will now!" He spoke up. "I thought you were gone. Alcohol was the only thing that kept me from feeling so much guilt... and pain."

She let go of me as she held her hand out in which Dad took.

"Well, I'm here now, and we all need to talk..." She stared into Dad's blue-green eyes. "...but when you're sober," she added.

We both nodded in agreement. We definitely needed to talk. Nothing made sense anymore. But this, having my mom back in my life, was the best gift anyone could have given to me.

But how? How was she really here?

Chapter 10

Katherine's P.O.V.

"Do I dare disturb the universe?" I thought to myself.

When Prufrock had asked that question, was he as lost as I was?

One minute was all that was needed to change everything. Decisions and revisions held a hefty baggage on me, for whichever path I decided to take, time could be distorted and backed up. Perhaps... it could have been reversed?

I looked up into the vast sky before taking out the sandwich I had prepared prior to coming here. I was in my favorite spot again- the grassy hill that stood above everything. Well, not everything. It barely was high enough to hover over the city, but in my world, that city was everything.

It must be nice to be one of them.

All of the city folks had relatively average lives. Sure, they had problems and situations that they had to deal with in their own lives, but they had it easy. All they had to do was breathe. That was all that was expected of them.

After a couple of minutes, I finished the sandwich, before letting my fingers wander through the softness of the grass.

I then began thinking about Angelica, and how I had rejected her. When I told her that I thought it would be best for us to just be friends, I saw the hurt in her eyes, and it pained me to see her in pain. But, more so, it pained me knowing that I was the one who had caused that in her.

When I had said those words, I felt my whole body cringe, and my mind screamed that I had made a big mistake. In all honesty, she made me feel like I had a reason here on Earth. But, I knew my time here was not going to last for much longer. In fact, time was running out. Things were finally coming into place. She was slowly getting the life she deserved, which meant I was going to have to vanish soon.

And so, as you could imagine, saying goodbye to her would hurt us more if we were more than friends...

I just didn't want to live in agony for the rest of my existence.

So... how should I presume?

I came home to grade the papers from a quiz we had a few days ago. Everyone did fairly well, but, as always,

Angelica never failed to bring more to the table. Her strong use of vocabulary, and her diverse style of writing, use of description, and other advanced literary devices wowed me every time. The quiz she took couldn't even compare to the amount of knowledge that occupied her mind.

I leaned back on the couch and took a breath, as I decided it was time for a break.

Staring at the ceiling, all that filled my mind were memories and thoughts of Angelica.

"Aha." I chuckled a bit as I grabbed her hand and placed the paper between her fingers.

The class stared at us, and I could see the look in her eyes. It was filled with both anxiousness and embarrassment. She did not want to drop it again.

It was in that moment that she really got to notice me, and it was also in that moment that I got to see the side of her that was anxious around me. I thought it was cute.

I sat up on the couch and gently separated the graded and non-graded papers before placing them back in my case. I then opened the drawer that contained all of the movies I owned.

My eyes widened as they glanced upon a familiar one.

"How are you liking the movie?"

I shook my head as I pulled my hand away from The Princess Bride, though my mind continued to remind me of the memory.

"The movie is really pointing out the impossible... love prevails and conquers anything, but in real life, that is just a delusion..."

"I completely disagree." I spoke out loud, as if Angelica were in the room with me and could return my gaze, though she was obviously not here.

Realizing that, I shook my head in astonishment and decided that walking outside would clear my thoughts and allow me to stay in the now.

I sighed as I walked on the sidewalk in the middle of the night. It had to have been past nine, and the sky was filled with darkness. And, for some reason, tonight was the night everyone wanted to be out. Many were doing the same thing I was- walking. And maybe, they needed to clear their minds also.

It was starting to get a little chilly, and so I stuck my hands in my pockets before I felt something hard blocking one of my hands. I slipped the object out, and my eyes widened at the sight.

"I thought I left you at home," I mumbled as I glanced at my phone.

A smile quickly appeared on my face as a very familiar voice whispered in my ear.

"Let's take a picture together." The voice then said, "I never want to forget this moment."

"Are you sure that you won't forget?" I challenged. I then chuckled as I spoke again. "I don't believe you."

The voice suddenly became quiet, so I had figured it had vanished into the air. Too bad. It was nice having the company.

And, to my surprise, the voice spoke once more.

"Don't forget to smile," it reminded me.

I smiled in response. Mostly because I liked having the company again.

A neighbor eyed me and shook his head slowly, in disapproval. He must have thought I was crazy. I mean, I guess I was. I was walking in the pitch darkness and imagining a conversation. Even I would have smirked if I had seen myself in this moment.

I continued to walk, however, ignoring the stranger.

After about an hour had passed, I began to feel a bit weary. I then had this pounding in my mind, followed by the aching in my chest. My heart ached uncontrollably. At first, I thought it was due to all of the walking that I did, but I didn't walk for that long.

Just when I thought I had lost the voice that roamed through my head, it showed itself once again.

"Help me understand." It whined.

I held my head in my hands, and moaned softly as I tried to shake the feeling and the voice away.

"Be my teacher..." Those words sent shivers down my spine.

"Be... your... teacher." I restated to myself.

I pressed a hand on my chest as I realized who the voice had belonged to.

"I-I am trying, but I don't know how." I spoke, in defeat, knowing it was Angelica's voice I was responding to.

"You can't help me." The voice changed its mind.

The whisper then became louder and more audible.

"You aren't with me all of the time... you aren't with me when I'm at home."

The aching in my heart made itself more clear, and in that moment, a light bulb became lit inside of my head. Of course. Angelica needed my help. I must go to her now. I can't believe I had spaced myself from her this much.

I was Angelica's guardian angel, yet I had foolishly left her alone for a while.

"But... I can change that." I murmured to myself.

I began running down the narrow path, not paying any attention to the cold stares and the curious whispers that followed behind me. I had only one focus, and that was getting to Angelica and making sure she was safe.

That was one of my decisions, which had affected the realm that was ruled by time...

For Angelica's sake, I dared to disturb the universe; I dared to break the sequence, in hopes that there would be change- in hopes that our fates would change for the better.

CHAPTER 11

Angelica's P.O.V.

Cold hands skimmed the surface of my skin from head to toe. Her fingers lightly traced my scars, making me wince.

"Sorry."

Her eyes raised as she glanced at my face for a mere second.

"I'm sorry this happened to you, and that I was not here to prevent it."

Her voice was filled with regret and sadness. I tilted my head to the side as my eyes squinted.

"But, why? Why weren't you here, Mom?" I questioned. "Why weren't you here to protect me."

My tears streamed down my face, as my heart ached.

Mom kneeled down on her knees as her arms ran from my shoulders, stopping at my waist.

"Oh, Angelica. I wanted to. Believe me, I did."

She sighed as she stood up and grabbed Dad's and my hand. She then led us to the couch, where we sat. My mom, however, pulled a chair up in front of us, so that she could face us.

"But, I didn't have the strength or any determination left inside of me to want to stay here anymore."

Her eyes seemed to dilate as she began to tell us what had happened the night she disappeared.

"One night, I had a stressful day at work. My manager yelled at me, accusing me of pocketing the tips I had made..."

I arched a brow.

She was a waitress at a local restaurant called The Ruins, and it was a rule that all tips would be collected by the manager and the restaurant itself would keep forty percent of it all.

"Did you?" I questioned.

"Yes." She bit her lip, though didn't show any hint of self-disappointment. "But, I did it, because I needed the money."

"Why? We were not financially struggling." I retorted. I just didn't understand.

"True, but I had my reasons." She then eyed my dad, and I let my eyes wander to him as well. "When I got home, I noticed a trail of alcohol bottles leading from the front door and into the living room..."

Dad gulped as his head lowered. He was unable to maintain eye contact.

"I followed the path, knowing what I would see in the end. Your father was fatally drunk, once again. He sat on the kitchen floor, leaning against the refrigerator. Noticing me, he then tilted his head up, and looked at me, though his eyes revealed no evidence of actually being there or processing anything. 'Dance with me,' he pleaded as he tried to stand up. 'Dance with me, Clarise,' his voice was quivery, along with his shaky movements. I shook my head as I grabbed the bottle that was in his hand and placed it onto the counter."

Her eyes lowered slightly. I could tell she was having difficulty talking about this, just as it was difficult for me to hear it.

"An idea then came to me."

She gained back her confidence to continue.

"I was already having a bad day, and I was not feeling like myself. I was uncomfortable, angry, upset... confused, so I did something terrible. I figured that your father would be too drunk to remember anything, so I grabbed one of the kitchen knives and lightly scraped the palm of my hands and rubbed my blood on the sides of the knife and on his hands. I then grabbed his hand and placed the knife in it, and I walked out with both my purse and my secret stash of money in hand."

"W-what?"

What was I hearing right now? I've always and only had the image of my mom as the sweet, beautiful, and caring woman she was. She was the type of person that wouldn't even hurt a fly. My mind couldn't comprehend how a person like her could think of something this bizarre and selfish. In what world was that okay?

"Initially, my plan was to leave but take you with me," she told me. "But, I knew I didn't have enough money to support the two of us, so I had no choice but to leave you here with your father."

I frowned as I looked into my mom's cold blue eyes.

"There were different ways you could have gone about all of this. You shouldn't have left me."

Her eyes revealed her remorse as she responded with "I know that now."

"Why now? What made you finally decide that coming back was the right thing to do?"

A minuscule smile then appeared on Mom's face.

"As weird as this might sound, a stranger."

I looked at her, confused.

"A stranger?"

"Yea."

She chuckled, trying to bring joy into the broken room.

"Just the other day, I bumped into this mysterious woman, and she did the oddest thing. She just stared at me, and in her eyes, it looked as if she could see right through my soul. It was as if she knew who I was already."

"What did she say?"

I couldn't believe all it took was an encounter with a stranger.

"That I needed to go home and not avoid family issues. I just stared at her as I wondered what she had meant by her words. I knew she couldn't have known what my life was like because we had never met before that day, and there was no way I could have forgotten her face. She was quite beautiful and interesting."

"And, then what?" Dad chimed in.

"I just stood there, astonished." Mom admitted. "But then, I began to realize something. I left with the intentions, at first, that it was the right thing, but it resulted in the complete opposite. My mind said one thing, though my heart said another." She took a breath. "My mind deceived my heart," she acknowledged, nodding her head.

"You made me believe that I had killed you, Clarise."

There was evident pain in Dad's voice. He was hurting. I couldn't even begin to imagine how that must sting.

Mom patted him on the back, then moved her hand in a circular motion, in an attempt to comfort him.

"I know. And you didn't deserve that."

He lifted his head, glancing at my mom through his eyelashes. His eyes revealed pain, but something else. I couldn't really recognize that expression. It was different for him.

"No, Clarise," he began. "I didn't deserve you."

I gulped as I heard my dad saying those vulnerable words. He had really meant it.

"Don't say that. We all have some things we need to improve on in ourselves," she assured.

We both nodded as we listened intently. And, in what miraculous timing, the door flung wide open, startling all of us. Our heads swiftly turned, in response, and my eyes widened as I noticed who it was.

Katherine Hale.

I watched Katherine gasp for her breath. Had she been running in the rain all of this way just to get to me? I rushed over to her side and grabbed my jacket on the way. I wrapped her in it as I led her inside, closing the door behind her. She gave me a cheeky smile as she stared into my eyes, making me feel comfort in it.

"I'm here," she voiced, almost in a whisper.

"You're here," I repeated with the same cheeky grin.

I watched as her soaking blond hair straightened as some of the water dropped at the tips.

"And, you're soaking wet," I pointed out.

"I'm okay," she assured me, however, I didn't want her to catch a cold, and so I rushed into the kitchen, bringing back a towel.

"Aren't you afraid of catching a cold?" I wondered as I began wrapping it around her drenched hair.

"No. I was only afraid of not seeing you..."

Her eyes sparkled, sending me into a trance.

"Who is that?"

My mom squinted as she tried to make out who was at the door. My body was sort of blocking the sight of her. I gulped. What should I introduce her as? I couldn't tell her that my teacher was the one stopping by in the middle of the night. Right?

"That's Ms. Hale," my dad retorted. "Angelica's teacher."

I mentally cursed him for spilling that information out like that. I had almost forgotten that they'd met before.

Mom's lips formed an "o" shape, but, as she got a closer look at her, standing beside me, her jaw fell.

"You're Angelica's teacher?"

I arched my brow as I watched them interact with one another. Ms. Hale's grin widened as her eyes became inviting.

"Nice to be formally acquainted with you."

She stuck her hand out, which Mom took and gracefully shook.

"I'm glad you're here."

I was a bit confused at this encounter. Had they met before?

"Thanks to your much needed advice!" My mom cheered.

Ah, so She's the "mysterious woman" she was talking about earlier.

"Sometimes, we all need a little push to be brought back to reality."

Her eyes soon landed back on mine. It looked as if she was trying to confirm that I was okay that she had intervened. It was strange. Definitely strange. I told her that my mother was dead, yet she somehow knew that this woman was her at first sight. Maybe she was just very good at recognizing family resemblance. But, nevertheless, I was grateful that Katherine went out of her way to help make this happen.

"Yes, well please come in. We were just talking, but I need to make dinner anyway." My mom beamed.

"It's almost ten," I remarked.

Katherine smirked as she felt amused at my squealing.

"Nonsense. A late dinner is better than no dinner at all," Mom responded with delight in her voice. I guess she had a point.

"Yea, I should definitely eat something." Dad smirked.

He was slowly growing more comfortable in his skin, and more content. It made me happy to see that.

"Your food has always been amazing!" He complimented her.

My mom blushed as she skipped into the kitchen. It was crazy how fast things shifted tonight. It went from chaos to peace in what felt like an instant. And, best of all, Katherine was here. The one person who made my heart lift and flutter, the one who showed me the light, though all I could see was the darkness; the one who made my eyes gain back their sparkle.

I was undeniably falling for her, if I hadn't already.

CHAPTER 12

Little glances. That's all that was needed for us to communicate our admiration. My parents were oblivious. They chatted among each other about random trivial things, which Katherine and I pretended to listen to, and of course, we participated in the conversations, but our minds were never with them. I couldn't stop thinking about her, and wanting to scoot next to her, or whisper in her ear and say something sweet, bringing her to smile. And, I knew she felt the same way.

Because of her staring.

You see, your eyes communicate far more than what we anticipate sometimes.

"Angelica." I heard my mom's voice in the back of my mind. "Angelica." It became more clear.

I shook my head as I squinted, looking at my mom.

"Um. Yes?"

Katherine smirked as she wiped her lips with her napkin.

"She wanted to know how you liked the meatloaf," Katherine informed me.

I let out a faint giggle as I felt my cheeks redden due to my embarrassment. I knew I was zoning out, but I didn't realize I had completely tuned out my mother.

"It was amazing. You really do make the best meatloaf." I recovered.

"Doesn't she?" My dad agreed before leaning over the table to give my mom's lips a peck.

Almost instantly, I felt my eyes wandering away from the sight of them and landing back on Katherine. And, to my surprise, her eyes were already focused on mine, causing me to suddenly become nervous.

My eyes widened as they stared intently into Katherine's mystical-blue ones. I couldn't break the stare, though I wanted to look away. Her eyes revealed lust and yearning, yet she was trying so hard not to act on it. So was I. I gulped as her hands gripped the sheets as she looked down at me. I felt her legs brushing slightly on the sides of mine as she positioned herself over me. I felt my heart pounding in my chest as I wondered what was going on through Katherine's mind in that moment. When she came into the room, she didn't say a word. Instead, she climbed on top of me and just stared at me. All she did was stare. It was as if she was debating on something in her head. It was as if she wanted to kiss me, but tried, with every nerve in her body, to resist the temptation.

My bottom lip slowly separated from the upper as I struggled to let any words flow through them. I then noticed Katherine's eyes narrowing towards them, hungrily. Her stare began to be intoxicating, making it harder for me to breathe.

I gulped as I closed my eyes, in fear that I would make the wrong decision. If I were to kiss her in that moment, there was a possibility that she would reject it and be disappointed in me. Just the slightest possibility of her being upset with me, was enough to convince me to hold in my urges.

Though it was extremely difficult.

But then, warmth ran through me as Katherine's soft lips locked onto mine.

"Is this why she came over?" I thought, dwelling in confusion. Has she changed her mind about us only being friends?

Whatever the reason, I didn't question it. I just enjoyed every single second that we shared kissing on my bed. I felt her hair through my fingers as I held her close to me. I felt the warmth of her body, as my hands ran down her back. The kiss became very passionate very quickly. We've both had to hold our urges in for so long that one kiss triggered all of it. All of the longing. All of the yearning.

"Katherine," I spoke in between kisses.

Ignoring me, she trailed kisses down my neck, sending shivers down my spine. She was making it almost impossible for me to speak. My hand traveled up to her shoulders, holding onto them, as her kisses became more empowering.

"K-Katherine," I panted.

Her lips curved into a smile as her head popped up to look at me.

"S-sorry."

She bit her lip, shame reaching behind her eyelids.

"I tried to resist..."

That shame soon influenced her body, convincing her to crawl off of me. She settled for lying beside me, instead, her eyes never having left mine.

I shook my head as I leaned on my side, facing her. We just stared at each other for a while, seeing through each other's soul, and admiring each other's company. In that instant, time and space were irrelevant. Only her. A thought then came to me.

"Katherine," I whispered, once more.

Her eyes seemed to sparkle as she continued to gaze at me.

"Yes?" She spoke softly.

"Why are we doing this to ourselves?" I questioned.

In all honesty, I knew why. I knew exactly why, but for some reason, I couldn't help but feel like that was not enough. Being friends with her was not enough.

Her smile faded a bit as she sighed.

"Angelica..."

Something came over me as I covered her mouth with my hand, stopping her from speaking any further. Her eyes widened, the look of shock in her eyes. It was out of my character to do what I was about to do next, but in that moment, I didn't want to go on without my feelings being known.

"I love you," I confessed.

I felt the whole world falling silent as the most important three words flowed through my lips.

Katherine's eyes widened before squinting at me as my words had affected her.

"I love you more than words could ever show, and I think about you more than you could ever know."

I then breathed over her ear, sending shivers throughout her body.

"I've never loved anyone the way I love you. You're my everything."

Katherine's P.O.V.

I looked at her with my hurt eyes, yet I smiled, masking the hurt. Sad, wasn't it? It was a very sad thing that she wouldn't remember any of this. I guess the only thing I could have done was be honest with her. That's the least I could have done.

She stared into my eyes as she became vulnerable, anticipating my response, and so I gave her one.

"I love you too, Angelica," I managed to say before a tear streamed down my cheek.

She just stared at me dumbfoundedly, half smiling.

"No, Katherine," she then wiped away my escaping tear, with her thumb. "This is a good thing," her voice became slightly higher as it became clear she was now fighting against the tears that had wanted to stream down her face. "We're meant to be together," she believed.

We are. There was no doubt about that. I smiled light-heartedly, as I cupped her face in my hands.

"Are you happy now?" I needed to know she would be okay. "Your dad agreed to stop drinking and get help, your mom has returned, and Nathaniel is not bothering you anymore."

She pondered over what I had just said. Then, her eyes lit up, causing me to smile.

"And, it's all because of you, Katherine. You literally saved me..." She began to whisper before she wrapped her arms around my body, embracing me.

I guess she will be okay.

All that I had wanted was for time to freeze in that instant. I wanted to be in her arms forever, knowing she would be with me for eternity.

But, she will find me...

CHAPTER 13

I squinted as I lifted my eyelids, allowing the light to reach them. I then smiled as a familiar scent filled the room. I turned my head to the side and stared at the beautiful woman beside me.

"You're awake," Katherine smiled as she placed a tray of breakfast in between us.

I arched a brow.

"Did you make this?" I wondered. Awe, how sweet.

"I did."

Her eyes lit up with pleasure.

I glanced at the amazing meal before me, consisting of bacon, eggs and mashed potatoes. I then redirected my gaze on Katherine's gorgeous face.

"Thank you."

I bit my lip, prior to pushing the food to the side, making a pathway for me to reach her. I then crawled into her lap and wrapped my arms around her slender body.

She returned my embrace, sending a comforting warmth through me.

A smirk became apparent on my face as I gained confidence.

"The food was getting in the way."

"Was it?"

Katherine laughed before tickling my sides, inflicting my laughter.

"Hey, stop it!" I squealed.

Katherine's smirk widened with pleasure.

"Or what?"

"Or I'll..." I paused as I pondered over what to say next.

I couldn't think of anything so I just said what any child would say in that moment.

"Or I'll tell my mom!" I smirked.

She just looked at me, furrowing her brows, amused by this.

"Such a child," she remarked, finally releasing me.

I giggled softly before tilting my head back slightly, gazing into Katherine's icy eyes. She returned my stare, her eyes revealing her affection. It was nice. It was nice that I had someone like Katherine in my life. She was like my guardian angel. Ever since she was given to me, my life slowly turned around. Because of her, I learned what happiness was again.

It was because of her...

My lips curved into a smile as I leaned in closer, admiring Katherine's beautiful complexion. Her eyes sparkled, filled with delight, as she stood there, seemingly curious. Maybe she was curious about what I was thinking.

My heart seemed to skip a beat, as I leaned closer to her face. I felt the heat rushing to my cheeks as my lips pressed against her cheek. I lightly brushed it as if she were a delicate flower, causing her to smile from ear to ear.

"Hmm," she hummed, her angelic and gentle voice sounded in my ears, making my heart flutter.

We could do this all day. Just staring into each other's eyes, and expressing our admiration.

But then, a thought came to my mind. My teacher was in my bedroom, and my parents were just downstairs. How was this even happening? How was it real?

I slid my hand next to hers and eloped her pinky with mine, teasing her at first, before our fingers intertwined.

It was like we were stuck in a fantasy, a dream that I couldn't wake up from.

Suddenly, however, I heard my door squeaking, signaling me that someone was trying to come in. My eyes enlarged, as my anxiousness overwhelmed me.

I looked into Katherine's eyes, seeing her reciprocated fear.

"Katherine," I whispered, panicking. "What do we do?"

Before I knew it, the door flung open, revealing my mom. I gulped as she made her way towards us.

I watched her eyes shift from mine, and then, almost immediately, towards Katherine. She then did something that surprised me. She smiled. She didn't say a word at first. She just smiled, making me question everything. Was she approving of my teacher being in my bedroom? Was she possibly half awake? I didn't get it.

Her bottom lip, then, separated from the upper, as she searched for what words to say. What does someone say after seeing something like this?

"Ms. Hale..." I heard Katherine's name, playing on her lips, as she stared at Katherine for what seemed to be for eternity.

I was beginning to feel uneasy.

"I'm glad you slept over."

I arched a brow as my jaw dropped. She knows!

"How was your night?"

"Mom!" I immediately shrieked. "It's not like that!"

"Yea..." Katherine stood up, off of the bed, as she continued to look into my mom's eyes. "It was getting late, and it was pouring... Angelica insisted that it would be safer to stay, rather than to leave." She then looked at me as she continued with, "She's such a sweetheart."

My mom's grin widened as she nodded her head.

"She is."

Katherine's eyes then enlarged as my mom's arms began wrapping around her.

"It's okay." It's okay? "Stay as long as you like."

Mom then glanced at me as she released Katherine from her abrupt embrace.

"She's a keeper," I heard her say, in approval.

I couldn't believe what my mom was saying right now. She was being so supportive of this, though a regular parent would have been concerned, for many reasons. But still, I couldn't help but smile over all of it.

"She is," I felt my voice softening.

My mom's arms then pulled me into their embrace as her voice ran through my ears. There was a kind of intensity in it.

"I found your wallet," she informed me.

My eyes widened as they then wandered to the wallet that she was holding.

"W-what? H-how?"

I had almost forgotten that it was missing. At first, I began to wonder if my dad was the one who took it from me, in order to buy more alcohol. But then, I just kind of accepted the fact that it might actually have been lost.

Mom redirected her gaze at Ms. Hale as she then said, "It's a touchy subject..."

Katherine's eyes widened, followed by her nodding. I looked at her with worried eyes. Whatever it was my mom had to say, I didn't want Katherine to leave.

Without a second thought, I reached out for Katherine's hand, preventing her from leaving.

Her eyes dilated as she stared into my eyes.

"No," I breathed. "Katherine can stay."

I watched as Katherine's lips curved into a smile, hearing my warming words, as my hand remained in hers. I didn't want to let her go.

My mom nodded, wearing a knowing expression on her face, causing me to mentally facepalm. I said "Katherine", didn't I? Rather than Ms. Hale. If she didn't already, she definitely knows now.

"Okay. Well, I'm just going to say it."

She swallowed a proverbial lump in her throat as she pressed the wallet on the palm of my free hand. I grasped it tightly as I continued to stare into my mom's blue eyes.

"Your dad, actually, handed it to me, and told me that he kept it in one of his drawers."

I felt my brow twitching, hearing her words.

"S-so my assumptions were right..."

I lowered my eyes toward the sheets of the bed, feeling uninterested in hearing the rest of the story. What more was there to say? His actions couldn't be justified. And, worse of all, he wasn't even here to claim that he did it nor apologize for it. Unbelievable.

I hope the alcohol was worth it.

I suddenly felt Katherine's warm hand tightening her grip on mine, squeezing it, in an attempt to comfort me. But, I didn't look up right away.

My mom watched this, at first, in silence, but she soon continued.

"Your dad... he had the saddest eyes. He felt terrible for what he had done, and I could tell he regretted it."

"Where is he?" I heard myself say, in a voice that didn't quite sound like my own.

My mom's brows furrowed as she gave me a questioning look.

"Angelica?"

"Why isn't he here apologizing for what he did? I worked hard for that money," I made clear. My voice then became soft as I finished with, "I'm not mad. I'm just disappointed..."

"I'm sure he didn't mean to hurt you, Angel," Katherine assured me. "He was in a bad state. Sadness does strange things to some people."

I shook my head, in disbelief. Why was she defending him?

"Don't defend him, Ms. Hale."

Her eyes widened as she heard her last name playing on my lips. I then covered my mouth, feeling immediately sorry that I let that accidentally slip out. I knew it would hurt her feelings, hearing me address her so formally, as if we weren't something so much more. My mom seemed to understand the change in environment in the room as well, and so, she stood up and excused herself.

"I'll be in the living room," she vocalized.

She then jerked her head towards me as one foot stepped out of the door.

"I know how pure your heart is, Angelica. Don't let what your father did mess with your ability to forgive." She then light-heartedly smiled. "We love you, unconditionally, and we'll get back on track."

I returned her halfhearted smile as she closed the door behind her.

"Forgive me." I then said, in a whisper, as we were now alone, though Katherine never once let go of my hand.

Her expression seemed so warm, though I was so cold to her just a second ago. Unintentionally, but I still felt terrible about it.

"No. Don't be," she dismissed my apology. "There's nothing to forgive. You're absolutely perfect, Angelica."

She wore that soft, warm smile of hers that would mend any broken heart.

"Even angels are capable of feeling hurt, sometimes."

I nodded as I practically jumped into her arms, once more, enjoying her warmth.

"I'm glad you're here, Katherine. I can't seem to ever stay upset whenever you're around. You always know what to say to lift one's spirit."

She grinned, as she tightened her arms around mine.

"I love you."

I felt heat rushing to my cheeks as her words repeated in my mind.

"I love you too."

Katherine's P.O.V.

"Slow down!" I squealed, trying to catch my breath.

"Speed up!" I heard her say as she continued to run laps back and forth in the pool. She was fast. Too fast.

I grinned as I breathed for air, prior to diving underwater again, sneaking my way towards her. When she swam my way, I jumped up, out of the water, and caught her by the stomach.

Her eyes widened, before she let out a small laugh.

"How did I not see that coming?"

My grin widened as she then grabbed for my waist as she pulled me into a kiss. Our lips rhythmically moved in sync, heat rushing through me. I felt my heart pounding against my chest as I began to wish that we could stay in this moment forever. I couldn't help but smile as her lips continued to explore mine. Eventually, after a couple of minutes, she pulled away, leaving me in a trance. I didn't want it to end, though we had been kissing for a while. You see, when you love someone so much, you begin to miss every single thing about them, even when they're still there beside you. That's when you know you've found your soul mate.

"Had enough?" I teased.

She curved her lips into a smile, grinning from ear to ear, as she shook her head.

"No," she asserted. "I just needed to breathe."

"Well, if you-"

She wrapped her arms around my neck, and pressed her lips against mine, stopping me from finishing my sentence.

"Shush," she played, holding a finger against my lips, before placing her lips back on mine. When did she get so playful? I liked that side of her, though I liked everything about her. I mean, what was there not to love? She was adorable.

Angelica's P.O.V.

We had spent the rest of the day browsing the mall, and then, meeting my parents at a restaurant they had picked out. It went surprisingly very well. They were so approving of the relationship that Katherine and I had, which made my heart flutter. It felt nice that I didn't have to hide our relationship from them.

And, Dad even apologized directly to me over the whole wallet situation.

"I hate myself for hurting you, Angelica," I could hear the honesty in his voice. "And, I don't know if you've noticed, or not, but whatever money I had spent, I replaced it, plus more."

That was sweet of him. It showed me that he had really meant it, that he really was sorry. It takes more than just words to truly express an apology. It also takes action.

"I should get going now," Katherine informed me, making me feel sad.

But, I understood. After all, we practically had spent the entire day together.

"I need to finish grading some papers before tomorrow. Though we've had this Tuesday off, I decided to spend it with you, because you're my girlfriend."

I couldn't help but smile from ear to ear after hearing her say that. I was her...girlfriend.

"But, I'm also a teacher, who should be on top of this." True. She had to leave, though I wished she didn't.

"Okay," I nodded, understanding. "But..." I grabbed my phone out of my pocket. "I'd like to take another picture with you, along with my parents."

And, there it was again. That expression filled with uncertainty and sadness, though she put up a facade as she smiled at me. I didn't understand it. Did she just not like pictures?

"Sure," she still complied.

My parents walked towards us, joining us in the front yard, as I snapped the photo, with a bit of hesitation.

"Oh, that turned out great!" My dad approved, as they gathered around me, glancing at the picture.

"A nice family photo," I heard my mom say, which got Katherine to grin, earnestly, though I could still see through it.

Her grin was hiding something else. I just didn't know what it was yet.

I shut my phone off and placed it back in my pocket as I pierced my eyes into Katherine's icy-blue ones. I then heard the front door closing behind my parents, and so I had decided to confront her about it, about what it was that was consistently bothering her over the pictures.

"Katherine." Her eyes lit up, having her full attention on me, and so, I continued. "You're smiling..."

"Of course I am," she said, matter-a-factly.

"Then why do I feel as if it's only a facade?"

I leaned my face closer towards hers, as I studied her expression. She looked at me with saddened eyes. It was becoming increasingly difficult for her to keep her walls up, when all I was doing was bringing them down.

"I've got to go, Angelica," she spoke, dismissing my comment.

I watched her, in complete confusion, as she then walked towards her car.

"I'll see you tomorrow at school."

I watched her drive off, shaking my head. Why wouldn't she tell me? I needed to know what was going on with her. She had done so much for me. And, it was my turn to help her...

CHAPTER 14

"The time has come for me to leave, Angelica. But, don't worry." The woman looked at me, eyes filled with honesty.

"We will see each other again..."

Something seemed to change, her expression... it seemed to hold a kind of darkness.

"You won't even miss me," I then heard her say.

My eyes widened as her words replayed in my ears. How could she even say that? How could I not miss her? I held onto her arms, though the bright light above us began glowing with more intensity.

"Angelica..."

"Don't leave me!"

I held tighter onto her arms, using every ounce of strength that I had in order to prevent her from being taken away. A tear then stroke my cheek as her arms began slipping away slowly.

"Don't you dare leave me!" I squealed.

Her legs began to hover over the ground, slowly rising, yet I didn't let go.

"Why was this even happening?" I thought.

Fate had brought us together just to tear us apart.

The universe can be so cruel.

Her eyes beamed with rays of light shining through them. I watched as the angelic being rose, ready to go back to her home. Her lips curved into a smile, though a tear marked with sadness crossed her face.

"Remember me."

I looked intently in her radiant blue orbs.

"How could I forget-"

"-You?"

My eyes immediately opened as my heart pounded against my chest. A tear trailed its way down my cheek, a tear marked with a strange sense of reminiscence. I felt the sweat forming on my forehead, as my body was still shaking due to the fear my nightmare had caused.

Why was I having these dreams? They felt so real. And, the angel... I think it was Katherine.

The dream was all a blur, however. I could see the images in my mind, yet my brain couldn't quite comprehend it.

"Don't..."

I slowly took the covers off of me.

"...leave me," my lips seemed as if compelled or trained to say those words. Don't you dare.

I then felt this urge to walk towards my dresser, and so I did, not rejecting the sudden yearning. I felt the knob in between my hands, as I pulled the top drawer open. My eyes, then, gazed at what had remained in it, my photo book.

I felt the book under my fingers as I brushed it gently. Katherine has always hated photos. I could see it in her eyes. She wouldn't admit it, but she didn't have to.

I opened the book and allowed my eyes to scan the photos once more as my mind still pondered over everything.

What is it you're not telling me..?

Ring. Ring.

I pulled out my phone and looked at the caller I.D.

Jack.

"Hello?"

"Ah, Angelica. My, isn't your voice just beautiful over the phone."

I smiled as I stood in front of the closet, my eyes conceiving the magnificent green dress that Katherine Hale had lent me.

"Thanks!" I responded.

I felt my cheeks reddening as I pictured how I would look in the dress, but more so, I was imagining the comfort, knowing that Katherine had once worn it. It smells like her. She always had this distinctive flowery scent, like an orchid.

"Are you still there, Angel?"

"Yes."

I shook my head, realizing I was zoning out of the conversation and getting lost with the mere imagination of Katherine. I was so hopelessly in love.

"Oh, alright! It just seemed as if you weren't for a second there." He paused for a moment, then continued. "You became quiet." He observed.

"I guess I was..."

A smile became apparent on my face, which I felt like Jack noticed, because he commented with, "What were you thinking about?"

I could hear him grinning as his voice then changed.

Me?" He had assumed.

I let out a light chuckle. "I'm looking at my dress right now," I informed him. "You do have the matching tie and corsage, right?"

"Of course I do, Darling."

Judging by the sound of his voice, he must had been smiling.

"I can't believe Ms. Hale just gave it to you like that. You must have been her favorite student!"

Oh, Jack. I was more than that. I grinned from ear to ear as I slipped on the green dress. It came down to my heels and formed my body quite nicely. I then hugged myself, imagining Katherine's warmth.

I smiled as I continued to embrace my body, with Katherine in my head.

"What are you doing over there, humming like that?" He smirked.

My eyes then widened. For a moment there, I had forgotten that I was on the phone with him.

"Should I come over there?" He teased.

"No!" I squealed, probably startling him. I then recovered as I finished with, "I want you to be surprised once you see the dress."

There was silence on his end, which made me feel a bit uncomfortable. Did I say something wrong?

"Fair enough," he finally told me, allowing me to breathe. "I can't wait to see my babe tomorrow."

I felt my body clenching at his words. "My babe"?

"I'm not your babe," I lightly chuckled, teasing him.

"Yet," he played.

I rolled my eyes at his comment. If only he knew that there was no possibility of us being more than just friends. I probably should make that clear. It wouldn't be fair to him if I had led him on.

"Well," I exhaled. "I'm going to hang up now."

"No, wait!"

I let out a nervous giggle.

"What?"

"Ah, nothing," he chuckled. "I just wanted to hear you talk once more before you hung up."

"Awe, Jack would make a great boyfriend to someone one day," I thought.

He was the perfect guy.

Just not the perfect guy for me.

"Okay, well I guess I'll just see you tomorrow then, if not today," I asserted.

"Yes, you will! Pick you up at six forty-five? We can get a quick bite to eat before prom actually starts."

I nodded. "Yea. Sounds great! See you then."

"See you then."

I shut my phone off and slipped it in my pocket, when a knock sounded on my door.

"Who is it?"

I walked towards the door and rested my hand on the doorknob. There was no response, which made me curious. Who is at the door? I slowly turned the knob, revealing nothing.

No one was there.

Huh, strange. I was probably just hearing things, so I had just completely erased the thought in my mind.

I then took off Katherine's dress and put on a plain black t-shirt, blue jeans and a hoodie. I then searched for my wallet. There it is. I grasped the wallet in one of my hands as I placed it in my bookbag.

It was time to go to school...

I walked around the corner and spotted Katherine's classroom. She wasn't standing outside of the door greeting her students like she usually did, which made me a bit disappointed.

It was always nice getting a greeting from her before class actually started.

I walked in and sat in my usual seat in the front, paying no particular attention to any of my classmates. I placed my book bag beside my desk, and then, tilted my head up to get a glance at Ms. Hale, who was sitting at her desk, marking papers.

"Ah, that's why," I thought. She was still behind in grading. I understand now.

"Angelica..."

My eyes widened as I heard a familiar, but not particularly pleasant, voice behind me. I turned around to face who the voice had belonged to. He grinned as he stared at my hoodie.

"Nice hoodie," Nathaniel complimented.

He then paused as he stared at me, seemingly debating in his head on what he would say next.

"Are you excited for Prom?" He asked.

I stared into his eyes, which revealed none other than honesty and realness. Maybe he truly had come around. It made me happy to see that he was trying to be a better person, the person I knew he could be.

"Yea, it's going to be a blast," I grinned from ear to ear as I squinted.

Nathaniel's smile widened, though he seemed like he was a bit awkward in his own skin talking so casually and pleasantly towards me.

It was definitely new to him.

He then cleared his throat as his eyes wandered around the room. After seeing that no one was paying much attention to us, he exhaled, releasing some of the tension he had. He looked at me with his chocolate brown eyes.

"You're going with Jack, right?"

"Yea." I bit my lip. "But, only as friends." I had to make that clear.

Ms. Hale was only a few feet away from me, and I didn't want her to get the wrong idea.

In my heart, there was no room for Jack, because it was already reserved... for Katherine.

He lightly chuckled.

"I see."

"Okay class," Ms. Hale walked around her desk and wrote something on the board.

I squinted as I tried to make it out. She then turned around to face us as she continued.

"As you all know, tomorrow is a big day for you seniors."

Cheers and hollers almost immediately sounded in the room as the students became overwhelmed with excitement. I smiled at the sight.

Ms. Hale stared at the students, also seemingly amused. She then separated her bottom lip from the top as she waited for the class to settle down.

"Well..."

A small grin became apparent on her beautiful face.

"I'm not going to be the kind of teacher that would give you all so much homework the day before. I know that you all need the day to make last minute preparations..."

"And, that's why you're the best!" Kyle beamed.

"Hot and fun."

One smirked, causing my brow to twitch ever so slightly.

"How can we ask for more?"

"W-will you be there..?" A shy boy spoke up, out of curiosity. "...M-Ms. Hale?"

He gulped as he waited for her response. Asking a question seemed to have taken so much out of him.

And, to think that used to me.

Ms. Hale smiled as she nodded her head.

"I was asked to be one of the chaperones."

I felt my heart flutter due to my excitement, and I couldn't help but smile from ear to ear. Katherine was going to be there, which meant I could possibly hang out with her and talk to her. I would at least be able to stare at her and admire her from afar. It was going to be great!

The bell had rung, signaling that class was now over. We had a free day to finish up late work, if we had any, or to talk quietly among ourselves.

I slid my book bag over my shoulder, as I walked towards Ms. Hale. She remained at her desk, her eyes glued to some papers, paying no attention towards me at first.

I cleared my throat.

"Ms. Hale..."

I watched as Katherine's head tilted up, and as a small grin became plastered on her face.

"Angelica..."

She bit her lip, before glancing at the now empty classroom. Her eyes then lit up as she walked around her desk and towards me.

I stared into her ocean-like eyes, admiring the beauty in them.

"Your eyes..."

I felt my eyes dilating as I focused harder on them.

"Have they always looked so beautiful?"

She smirked as she looked intently at me.

"Have you always been this adorable?" I heard her say.

Katherine's words made my heart flutter.

My eyes then gained a spark to them as I scanned my body with a small devious smirk plastered across my face.

"Yea..." My smirk widened. "...I would like to think so."

I winked, which caused her to laugh.

We both laughed together, which was nice. It was nice hearing her laugh again. It was a reminder that I made her happy somehow. It was comforting to know that I had caused that laugh in her... or when she would smile.

I've always loved her smile.

I then whispered, breathing into her ear.

"Katherine..."

I watched as her eyes enlarged, anticipating my continuing.

"So, you're going to be at Prom," I confirmed.

She nodded, though her mind seemed elsewhere in that moment. I bit my lip as I pondered over what to say next. I felt my jaw lowering, though there was nothing more for me to say.

I then felt a kind of pressure on my lips as Katherine's finger shushed them.

"Will you come visit me at the stands?"

Her lips curved into a smile as her eyes revealed something. Happiness. Though it was bittersweet.

I smiled, matching hers, as I responded.

"Of course I will, Ms. Hale."

CHAPTER 15

"**S**weetie, do you need help putting on the dress?"

Another knock.

"Angelica... um, yea. You need help with that?" A masculine voice sounded in the room.

"Angelica Rose, are you even listening?" My mom knocked again, making my ear drums burst. "Angelica."

I twisted the knob of my bedroom door and opened it quickly. Their eyes locked onto mine, after glancing at my dress.

"Wow..."

My dad's eyes roamed at the creases of the dress, following its pattern.

"You look..." His eyes widened. "You look beautiful."

My mom's eyes sparkled as a grin became plastered onto her face.

"My daughter is all grown up."

Her smile began to be intoxicating with how wonderful and genuine it looked. It had caused me to return that smile as they brought me into their embrace.

My dad's expression changed a bit, from an amazed one to a protective one.

"Now where's this boy that's accompanying you?"

I smirked as I scratched my head.

"His name is Jack, and he's actually a really nice guy..."

He raised a brow.

"Isn't he a football player?"

He leaned in closer, his eyes beginning to communicate something on their own.

"What did I say about football players, Angelica?"

"I know. I know," I exhaled as they finally released me from the hug. "But, he's different. You know, Daddy, it's never good to believe in ridiculous stereotypes."

He light-heartedly grinned as his eyes softened with his stare, revealing that he was actually listening.

"I guess I shouldn't assume until I meet him..."

He let out a miniscule chuckle, prior to his smile widening.

"Though, I'll be keeping a keen eye on him. Boys are never up to any good."

Mom chucked as she eloped her hand with Dad's.

"Oh, Carl. Angelica is a good girl. I'm sure she can pick the right boys."

I remained silent, though a minuscule smile appeared across my face.

It made me curious though. My mom knew that Katherine and I were together, yet she was okay with me going to the dance with Jack, who was a boy. Was she allowing me to date two people at the same time? Then again, she also knew that Katherine was my teacher and that going to the dance with her was out of the question.

I guess she just wanted to see me having fun with someone my age, as well.

A couple of minutes had gone by, and before I knew it, the phone had rung.

My eyes enlarged as the hint of excitement ran through me.

"I'll get it!" I practically yelled as I skipped my way to the landline. "It's probably Jack."

"Your date?" Dad had assumed.

I nodded as my hand grasped the phone, but to my surprise, a different voice had greeted me.

"Angelica," a feminine voice ran through my ears, immediately making my body tingle due to my excitement.

I looked at my parents, who were seemingly invested in a conversation of their own, and so I alleged.

"Katherine," my lips curved into a smile. "How are you?"

"I'm great," she replied.

Her voice then shifted as she spoke some more.

"You didn't talk that much in school today, and you ran out of class before I could get the chance to speak to you..."

There seemed to be a hint of sadness in her voice. I guess she needed to talk to me.

"I missed you."

My smile widened as I felt heat rushing to my cheeks. Awe, she misses me?

"It's only been a day."

I bit my lip as my voice then lowered, though above a whisper.

"I missed you too..."

Katherine lightly chuckled, and even though I couldn't see her in person, in that moment, her voice alone gave me comfort.

"Don't forget to visit me in the stands."

"How could I forget?" I responded.

Honestly, seeing her was the only thing that ran through my mind. It would have been impossible for me to forget.

She chuckled once more.

"I'm just making sure..." She paused for a moment before continuing with, "I guess I'll see you soon."

"Yea," I giggled before tightening my grip on the phone, a warmth filling my voice. "Very soon," I then added.

"Goodbye, Angelica," I heard her say.

"Goodbye, Katherine."

I hesitantly placed the phone down, before leaning against the wall.

I couldn't wait to see Katherine. And, in complete honesty, I didn't want to end that call so soon. I could speak to her all day. She could never bore me. She was just that important to me. It got to the point where I began to feel empty without her. Whenever our conversations would end, or whenever we would part ways, I would feel as if a part of me had become weakened.

Katherine had enchanted me. She was my enhancement. With her, I was stronger and I felt complete. And, without her, I felt like a piece of me was missing.

She was my other half.

My better half.

I opened the front door as my parents stood close behind me, after hearing the doorbell ring.

Jack grinned from ear to ear as he held a bouquet of red roses in his hands.

"Wow."

He glanced at me from head to toe before looking back into my light blue eyes.

"You look beautiful."

I smiled as I accepted the rose he then handed me.

"Thanks, and you look handsome," I returned the compliment.

My dad rushed to my side as he began examining the roses that I had received.

"Red roses?" He remarked, more in a questioning manner.

He then stared Jack down, which made him gulp.

"Where are the chocolates, Son?"

My brow twitched as I began to feel embarrassed for him and for myself. Mom rested her hand "casually" over her mouth as she tried to hold in her smirk.

"U-um... they're... uh-"

Dad patted him on the back, roughly, but playfully.

"I'm just kidding, Boy," He had assured him, allowing him to breathe normally again.

"Oh..."

Jack's grin returned to his face as he then shook his hand.

"Well, it is nice to meet you, Sir." He then shook my mom's hand. "And, it's nice to meet you, Mrs. Rose," he stated as he then faced my mom.

"It's nice to meet you too," Mom beamed.

"Oh please. Call me Mr. Rose. 'Sir' makes me feel old," Dad retorted.

Jack nodded as mom freed his hand.

"Okay, Mr. Rose."

He then turned his head to face mine.

"Well, we better get going," Jack affirmed.

I nodded as I hugged my dad and mom once more.

"Take lots of pictures," Mom had wanted.

A glimmer of a smile had rested on my lips as I began unwrapping my arms from the two of them.

"I will."

CHAPTER 16

"Here's your punch, Madam," Jack deviously smirked, his eyes filled with excitement.

I lightly chuckled as I extended my hands out to retrieve the cup. I then smirked as I responded with, "Thank you, my good sir."

I took a few sips of the drink before Jack began to stare at me intently, making me wonder what was going through his mind.

"What?" I questioned.

"Nothing."

"You're staring at me." I decided to call him out for it.

I could see Jack's cheeks reddening as he became more submissive and uncomfortable. He then smiled as he extended his hand out in order to grab mine. My eyes widened due to his sudden touch, but I didn't flinch. Gaining back some of his confidence, he began to speak.

"May I have this dance?" He smirked.

I smiled as I then tightened my grasp of his hand, returning his energy.

"You may," I allowed.

We started dancing in sync and swaying our bodies with the music. It was all alluring, in a way. I had almost forgotten where I was for a moment. It felt like a place like no other. In all of its scenery, and in all of its persuasion.

I felt like I was floating beyond the clouds. Or, possibly... was I falling?

The flashing luminous lights, the blasting, yet pleasant, music, and all of the people...

Oh right. My eyes widened as I began to snap out of my self-induced trance. Where's Katherine?

I held on to Jack's shoulders as we continued to dance to the slow-paced song, though my eyes gazed around, wanting to find something, to find someone.

After the song had ended, Jack slowly backed up from me, as if not actually wanting to part, but knew that the song ending was a cue for the separation. He then looked intently into my eyes as he gave me one of his charming yet earnest smiles. His bottom lip then separated from the upper as he began to speak, not just from his mouth, but from his heart.

"You're beautiful..."

I looked at him with denial in my eyes.

"Stop," I rejected.

He shook his head, refusing to comply with my command.

"You're so kind and gentle. Like an angel, you could do no harm. And, you can dance..." he smirked on the last part, which made me smile. "I'm... I'm glad I asked you out."

I felt my heart dropping in my chest. I had to be honest with him.

"Jack-"

"Before you say anything," he interrupted. "I want you to have this."

He pulled, out of his pocket, a shiny silver necklace, and raised it up for me to see. My eyes widened as I stared at its beauty. I suddenly felt very guilty that he had bought it just for me.

"I noticed that you never wear gold jewelry..." He then paused before laughing at his next comment. "...or I guess any jewelry for the matter, but I thought silver would look nice on you."

I looked at him with sympathy in my eyes, which got him to raise a brow over his confusion. He was confused that I looked bothered over his considerate gesture.

"Jack," I sighed. "This necklace looks too nice for me..."

I stared at the ground, trying to recollect my thoughts. How do I even say this? I didn't want to hurt his feelings. He was too good of a person. He didn't deserve this. It was not fair that I had to bring him down; it was not fair that he had to be brought down by me.

"What do you mean?"

He was clearly puzzled.

"Sure you do."

There was still this kind of light in his eyes, which I knew would soon change after what I was about to say next.

"I-I don't," I asserted, my eyes lowering towards the ground.

I then locked my eyes on his, as I forced myself to have the infallibility to continue.

"It would look a lot better on Claire."

"Claire?"

"Yea. She was all over you for as long as I can remember."

I half-heartedly grinned, as sorrow continued to fill my eyes.

"She loves you."

Jack's eyes roamed elsewhere for a second before looking back at me, still consisting of his confusion.

"But... I love you." Gosh, that must sting.

I sighed as I lowered his hands, which still held onto the necklace.

"But, I don't. At least not the way you want me to."

I noticed how his expression quickly changed from astonishment to complete and utter despair.

"I love you, but in a friend sort of way. Or like a brother."

I had hoped those words would make him feel at least slightly better. It made me feel terrible that he was hurting.

"There's a part of me that wishes I could feel that way about you. Really, I do. But, it's just... it's just not there."

I bit my lip as I struggled against my fidgeting tears.

"I-I'm sorry. I really don't want to hurt you."

He let out a cavernous sigh as he half-heartedly smiled in my direction.

"But, you already have..."

There was an evident hurt in his voice, which made my heart cringe for him. I'm so sorry, Jack.

It was too late. A tear had won the battle as it crept down my cheek and dropped from my chin.

"I'm really sorry, Jack."

"Why did you even agree to go to this with me? Was I only second best?" He asked. His eyes then seemed to dilate as he continued with, "Did you only go with me, because you couldn't go with your real crush?" Wow. How do I even respond?

I cleared my throat, which seemed as if it had tightened on its own.

"Jack, it's not like that. I-"

"Angelica..." He cut me off as he raised his hand in front of my face, catching me by surprise. "It's not like I'm mad at you. I don't think I could ever be mad at someone like you. Like I said before, and I'll say it again. You are the epiphany of an angel. I know you didn't mean to hurt me. Yet, I am..."

He lowered his hand as he backed away slightly as his half-hearted grin widened ever so slightly, as if he had wanted me to feel comfort in it.

"But, I'll be okay. I just need to be elsewhere right now."

"I understand..." I sighed.

"Don't worry about me," he conveyed. "I'll see you on Monday, okay?"

My eyes seemed to dilate as his words flowed through my ears. He was so mature about this, and he was holding it together for me.

"Okay," I breathed.

He soon left my sight, leaving me with my paradoxical feelings. If Katherine hadn't come along, would I have liked him? Would things have been different? I shook my head at my thoughts as I began walking towards the stands. I shouldn't think about what could have gone differently. All I know right now is that I wouldn't trade this reality for any other.

Katherine was too special to me.

I stopped in front of the beautiful woman who was currently talking to one of her other students.

"Just have fun. This is your last prom. Don't worry about anyone else but yourself," she had advised.

The girl sniffled before a genuine smile crossed her face.

"You're right. Thank you, Ms. Hale," she obliged with gratitude.

"Anytime, Hannah."

Katherine's icy-blue eyes then locked onto mine as a brilliant smile greeted me. It immediately made my heart feel this sort of warmth, though it had felt cold just a second ago.

"Hello, Ms. Rose," she spoke with her warm and gentle voice.

"Hello, Ms. Hale," I mimicked as a cheeky grin became apparent on my face. "How's the stands?"

She handed me a cup after filling it up.

"It's alright. How's the dance? Are you and Jack having a fun time?" She had wondered.

I sighed as I lowered my eyes at the ground, remembering what had just occurred.

"We were..."

Her eyes were fixated on me as sympathy filled them.

"What happened?"

"I told him that I didn't love him the way he wanted me to," I swallowed.

She just stood there, pondering over what I had just said for a second there, but, soon after, her lower lip slowly separated from the upper as she began to speak once more.

"Well, you can't like everyone in the world who is fond of you. It's just how the world works. It's a good thing you were honest with him, and I know he will recover sooner rather than later," she informed me.

She always did have a way with words, and I knew she was right. Still, I couldn't help but feel bad about it, however.

"It just sucks..." I pouted.

Katherine placed a hand on my shoulder, in an attempt to comfort me as she smiled.

"Just know the time will pass. All of it won't matter later."

I tilted my head up as I looked at her strange distinctive expression which matched her shifting voice. She then turned away from me, causing me to become more curious over the matter. I couldn't help but feel as if she were talking about something else. Something other than my guilt about Jack.

Soon after, Katherine told me to go mingle with my peers, and so, I was practically forced to leave her presence, which made me feel strange. It felt weird separating from her, and I didn't want to. I wanted to spend time with her, not any of the kids at the school.

Nevertheless, I listened to her as I walked away.

An hour had gone by as I talked to many of my classmates, who actually seemed interested in our conversations as well. I was no longer discriminated against by them. I was just another classmate in their eyes. It was a nice feeling.

I then became curious about Jack's whereabouts, so I danced my way through the dance floor, eventually spotting him talking to Claire. I smiled as I heard them laughing together. Claire grinned from ear to ear as her cheeks reddened. It was clear she was having a great night, and I knew in that moment that Jack would be okay.

"What a night," I thought.

Prom was coming to an end, and so, I instinctively looked around for Katherine, but she was nowhere to be found. I first checked at the stands, but there was no sign of her, so I checked the dance floor next, which quickly became vacant. Again, she was not there. Where could she be?

I began to feel this knot in my chest. I was starting to feel as if something was wrong- as if something had happened to her.

I found myself walking outside in the darkness, and, as if compelled to do so by nature itself, I started walking towards a place where I had only seen in my dreams.

The wind harshly pushed the trees around and made the flowers cry out. One, in particular, had caught my eye. A white tulip. Those were surrounding me when I was here. I picked one up as I continued to walk through the enchanted place known as the meadows.

I was about to stop for air, when a figure became present from a distance from me. I squinted, as my eyes tried to focus on the shadowy figure.

My feet, on their own, traveled closer and closer towards it, and then it became clear to me that the image was of a

woman. She just stood there as if waiting for something...
or someone.

The storm seemed to not have a great effect on her, for
she remained in place on the grass.

I slowly lurked further, trying to get a better glimpse of
the woman.

My eyes then widened as a tear struck my face, due to a
bittersweet recognition mixed with confusion.

Why was she out here? All alone in the darkness?

CHAPTER 17

The darkness surrounded the two of us as we stood there in silence, listening to the wind. I gulped as I decided to confront her.

"Katherine?" I spoke, yet she didn't budge. "Katherine, is that you?"

I spoke up that time, though my body was shivering due to the cold harsh wind and due to my wavering nerves.

The woman seemed to have heard me. I knew she did. And, after a few seconds had passed, she slowly turned around to face me, with a smile on her face, though that smile appeared to be forged. What was going on?

"Katherine, what are you doing out here? It's dangerous."

My eyes seemed to dilate as I continued to look at her expressionless face, as if the storm was nothing at all.

"There's a storm."

I tried to warn her, but, again, she just gave me a blank stare, which made me become a bit irritated.

"Katherine..." I whispered as my heart began to frown. "...come here. Come to me."

I fixated my eyes on her lost ocean-like ones, and I began hoping that she would come to her senses. It really was dangerous to be out here right now. It was also kind of strange. There was no sign of a storm coming, yet here it was, with no hesitance to greet us.

Katherine stayed put, however, ignoring my request.

"Seriously? What is going on with her?" I thought. Fine. If she won't come to me, I'll come to her.

I slowly walked closer to Katherine to the point we were just inches apart. My jaw, then, dropped ever so slightly as something had caught my eye. I didn't notice this before, but her eyes...they were glowing slightly. They had reminded me of the moon's borrowed light shining on the sea. They looked so beautiful. I've never seen anything like it before. Such luminescence, such refinement. I then shook my head at my thoughts. Now was not the time for admiration. This was beyond strange, and it was scaring me seeing her in this kind of state. Something was clearly wrong with her.

"You're eyes," I mumbled.

She tilted her head to the side as she looked at me, curiosity filling her eyes.

"They're glistening," I continued.

"It's my true form," she finally spoke, in a voice other than her own.

It held more gentleness, and it echoed through the thin air. It was quite beautiful. So enchanting.

"What do you mean?" I questioned.

I didn't understand what was going on right now.

Her lips curved into a smile as she leaned in closer to me, to the point I could feel her breath on my chin.

"I was born with these eyes, Angelica," she began. "It means we need to talk..." Well, yea.

"Apparently, we do," I retorted.

She bit her lip as she reached out for my hands. I tightly grasped them as I looked intently into her eyes.

"Angelica, I have not been completely honest with you. I've been hiding the biggest part of myself."

I nodded as I listened intently. Whatever it was, she needed to tell me. It was worse to keep it to herself for any longer. She had always been acting weird. No matter what we were doing, or where we were, there would always be this other side of her, the side that she masked with a simple smile. There was always this side of her that held a kind of pain and despair. It appeared to be an unresolved kind of pain. Something had definitely happened to her, and she needed closure.

That was for sure.

But, what was occurring now? This had caught me off guard completely.

I looked at her with assuring eyes as I tried my hardest to speak very warmly, in hopes it would permit her to be completely honest with me.

"You can tell me anything, Katherine. I just want you to be safe, and I don't want you to feel like you have to hide any part of yourself from me anymore."

I tilted my head to the side as my breathing then slowed.

"I've noticed the way you looked in the photos. I could tell that you didn't like taking them," I began to confess. "At first, I didn't quite understand why, but then, everything else pointed to it. I noticed that you were in a lot of pain, perhaps from an unresolved conflict or situation that had occurred in your life. But, Katherine..."

I squeezed her hands, conveying my support through touch.

"You can tell me what's going on with you. I want to know. You've helped me get my life back. Let me help you get yours..."

A tear fidgeted its way down her face as she looked at my concerned expression.

"Angelica..." She muttered. "I was sent here to protect you. I was... I was your guardian angel."

I arched a brow. "B-but you're... you're my teacher."

What did she mean by that? All of this time, she would say that I should think of her as one, but I didn't ever expect her to say that she really was an angel.

"In this life, yes. I was," She nodded before staring at me, giving me an assuring look. She then wore a light-hearted smile as she continued with, "But, like a puzzle, your life is now complete, which, unfortunately, also means the time has come for me to leave, Angelica. But, don't worry."

Then she looked at me, eyes filled with honesty.

"We will see each other again..."

Something seemed to change, her expression... it seemed to hold a kind of darkness.

"You won't even miss me," I then heard her say.

I tilted my head to the side as her words replayed in my ears. It dawned on me that I've heard those words before. In my dreams. But now, more than ever, I've come to realize maybe those weren't really just dreams, but other realities that I've once experienced. Realizing what was happening, I held onto her arms, though the bright light above us began glowing with more intensity.

"Katherine, angel or human, whatever you are, it doesn't matter. To me, it doesn't," I began to speak. "All that I care about is that you stay in my life."

Tears, that I tried so hard to restrain, began streaming down my face now, as my vulnerability became known.

"Angelica..."

"Don't leave me!"

I held tighter onto her arms, using every ounce of strength that I had in order to prevent her from being taken away. A tear then stroke my cheek as her arms began slipping away slowly. "Don't you dare leave me!" I squealed.

Her legs began to hover over the ground, slowly rising, yet I didn't let go. I stared deeply into Katherine's truest eyes as my voice seemed to project on its own, though shattering at each word.

"I don't want to forget that I love you, and I don't want to forget that you love me!"

Her eyes beamed with rays of light shining through them. I watched as the angelic being rose, ready to go back to her home. Her lips curved into a smile, though a tear marked with sadness crossed her face.

"Then remember me..."

I looked intently in her radiant blue orbs. "I promise that I will." My eyes seemed to dilate as I tried to soak in this last moment with her. "No fate can choose how I feel or what I can remember. You will always be in my heart. I love-"

And time seemed to shift to a different dimension.

Katherine's P.O.V.

My hands slowly slipped out of Angelica's as I saw her saddened expression. Right before God had taken me away, she had sworn to me. She told me she would remember me. Though that was really sweet of her, we've been through

this cycle many times, and each time it ended the same.
With my aching heart and her forgetting about me...

I looked into the eyes of my master, though mine were
torn and lifeless.

He returned my gaze, seeing the hurt in my eyes.

"Katherine," he called out to me. I tilted my head up,
though it was hard to even do that. "Are you okay?"

A minuscule smile appeared onto my face, almost in
disbelief that he would ask that.

"I don't think I will ever be okay..." I heard myself say.

He nodded as the look of sympathy was apparent.

"Then why go on with this?" He asked, in confusion.
"Why continue to relive the past, when you could just settle for the present." His voice became more cavernous as
he stared at me intently, trying to understand. "Why put
yourself through this?"

My light glistening eyes seemed to lose a bit of its shine
as I breathed out. I tilted my head up, and closed my eyes.

"Because, I love her..."

My smile widened as the image of her had resurfaced in
my mind.

"I cannot rest and settle for this reality. My life is worth
nothing without her in it." I then looked back into God's
deepened eyes. "Don't you see? I may be hurting living the
way I am, but I would hurt far more living any differently."

I watched as he inhaled deeply and pondered over what I had said. He then nodded, as if beginning to understand the gravity of it all- the gravity of my love.

His jaw then wavered as I waited for him to respond.

"As you wish, my dearest angel..."

EPILOGUE

Floating... or was it falling?

Falling... or was I dying?

Light... I remember fearing it.

Dark... I would always see it.

Flashes... and memories.

Lost... and forgotten.

I swore...

Did I break it? Do you think I broke it?

I lifted my eyes, allowing the rays of light to reach them, though the light had already shown its identity.

In my dreams...

I then breathed out as realization didn't fail to greet me.

I was awake...

I hopped out of my bed and walked towards my closet, pulling out a sweater. It was Monday, which meant I had to start getting ready for school, though I didn't exactly want to.

The teacher didn't seem like she cared for anyone anyways. She would just give us nasty stares, telling us that she wished she got that "other position". Apparently, she got turned down, because the Principal believed that her presence might actually scare the students.

A minuscule smile had formed on my thin lips as I lightly giggled at the thought.

A half an hour had gone by, and I found myself lying on my bed again, looking up at the ceiling. My eyes dilated, as they got lost in the starry image from above.

I've always loved looking at the sky and the vastness of it. For some reason, I think I've always felt drawn to it.

There was just something about the sky that made me feel so at peace. So at home...

I then found myself walking towards my dresser, as if compelled to. I felt the sudden yearning to open up the top drawer and see what I had inside. My eyes widened as they landed upon a random book that seemed to occupy the entire space.

I grabbed the book, carefully grasping it in my hands, and I laid back down on my bed. I bit my lip as I slipped my fingers inside, opening the book to the first page.

It was a picture... of me. And only me.

I tilted my head to the side as I wondered where I was when I had taken it. It looked like I was in an ice ring because I could see a white round surface behind me that resembled ice. But, what made me curious was the fact that I had taken a picture of myself, all alone.

Was there no one with me? Did I really go alone?

My eyes then wandered at the empty space next to me. There was nothing there. No one.

I felt this aching feeling in my chest looking at that, looking at the emptiness as if something, or someone, had belonged there. I felt... sad. Though I didn't know why. Looking at that photo made me feel lost. I felt as if something were missing.

A tear struck my face as I had dwelled in both confusion and despair.

"What is it?" I thought in astonishment. Why am I feeling this way? I lifted my hands up and slowly wiped my tears away with my thumbs, though it was a hopeless act, for many more came, reminding me that I couldn't just ignore them- reminding me that I couldn't run from it.

I frantically flipped the pages, trying to find something. An answer. An explanation as to why I felt this way. My eyes seemed to enlarge, as hopelessness and darkness continued to fill them.

In each photo, I was alone.

There was no one. No one...

Even in the family photo, there was a gap, the size of a person, in between my mom and I.

I placed my hand over the image before brushing the vacant space of the image. I outlined it, trying to figure it out. The puzzle inside of my head. The missing piece. Where was it..?

"Angelica, Angelica," A familiar, though unpleasant, voice called out to me.

I sighed as I shoed him off with my hand.

Usually he would be persistent in his harassment, but this time was different. Instead, he furrowed his brows as the look of concern was written all over his face.

"Um... What's wrong, Ms. Rose?"

I turned around in my chair to face him before locking my eyes onto his.

"I don't... I don't know."

Nathaniel's expression that once imitated sympathy, and actual concern, changed into a mocking one.

"Seriously, Angelica?"

A minuscule smirk played onto his lips.

"And, this is why I don't show sympathy." He then grabbed his notebook and pretended to write something down, as he concluded with "lesson learned."

I exhaled as I turned around, facing the front.

"And, this is why I don't talk to you," I mumbled, under my breath.

It was unlike me to say those certain things, but I guess you could say I was not in the best mood that day. I woke up feeling terrible. I woke up feeling empty.

Maybe this was God's way of telling me that I needed to change and control things in my life.

Maybe God wanted me to find happiness.

I smiled at the thought.

"Pencils. Paper..."

I lifted my head up, as my eyes landed on our teacher.

"Heads up. Ears open!" She continued.

And may the lecture begin...

3 Weeks Later...

We started dancing in sync and swaying our bodies with the music. It was all alluring, in a way. I had almost forgotten where I was for a moment. It felt like a place like no other. In all of its scenery, and in all of its persuasion.

I held tighter onto Jack's suit, feeling his warmth. I let out a light laugh, after he spun me around, like a prince would do for his princess. I curved my lips into a smile and returned the act as he looked intently into my eyes.

"I'm glad..." He began, his stare holding gentleness and delicacy in it. "I'm glad that I asked you out, Angelica. You're the epiphany of an angel."

I squinted as I studied Jack's face. He was so sweet. People really did need to give football players more justice.

His cheeks then reddened, as he pulled out a silver neck-lace.

"I love you," he had confessed.

And, it was in that moment where I felt as if time had frozen. More so, I was frozen. Something in me changed. There was a storm brewing inside of me. A facade waiting to be knocked down. A heart...

A heart waiting for-

I stared into Jack's loving compelled eyes as guilt ran through me.

"I can't..." I heard myself say. "I can't love you."

He arched a brow in confusion as he slowly lowered the necklace that he once held up high.

"I don't understand."

"Neither do I," I acknowledged. "All I know is that I just can't."

I tilted my head up, looking at the ceiling, imagining the ominous sky and all of the stars within. My smile returned, before my lower lip slowly separated from the top.

"There's someone out there for me, and she's waiting for me..."

"Who?" Jack was astonished at the sudden news.

"I don't know that yet, but one day we will meet again."

I lowered my head in order to face Jack once more.

"And, until then, I must wait, for my heart is reserved for her."

I closed my eyes as I then placed a hand on my chest, where my heart would be, imagining my long lost lover.

It was just a hunch. Just a lingering hope. A wish, really. There was no evident sign that there really was someone. But, I felt it. I felt her presence in my heart.

I just knew she was out there somewhere.

My soul mate.

Jack slowly nodded as he tried to wrap his finger around all of this. I could only imagine how confusing and strange that had sounded to him.

"It's okay," he finally spoke.

I felt my eyes dilating as I listened intently to his every word.

"I respect that." His smile then returned as he continued with, "I respect that you have that kind of hope in someone someday."

He grabbed my hands as he placed the necklace in them. I felt my hand grasping it as he curled my fingers around it, for me, making me accept the gift. My eyes looked back into his, filled with shock.

"I just want you to be happy. That's all I hope for."

I smiled as I wrapped Jack into an embrace.

"You really are the perfect guy, Jack."

Jack tucked one of my loose strands of hair behind my ear.

"I hope I can find another perfect girl." He wore a soft, though confident, grin, showing his teeth. "But, it might be hard."

"You will," I had believed. He definitely deserved someone as amazing as he was.

4 Years Later...

Walking down the sidewalk, I found myself stopping in my tracks as my eyes couldn't help but stare at something, radiating with beauty. There was this hilly area filled with the vastness of flowers. They were mostly white tulips, my favorite kind.

I curved my lips into a smile as I skipped my way through the meadows and twirled around, surrounded by nature's gifts.

I closed my eyes as I then lied on the grass, feeling the texture within my hands.

Nature is beautiful, isn't it? The earth and all of its glorification. And, if you're truly listening, you could learn something new about yourself by getting lost in it.

Suddenly, I felt a warm hand sliding through mine, causing my heart to quicken. Our fingers intertwined, sending a familiar electrical current throughout my body, as if completing a circuit. The figure lied on top of me, yet was careful to position theirself. It was evident that the figure did not have any intentions of hurting me.

And, before I knew it, I felt soft lips locking onto mine as I remained there in shock. At first, I did not know how to react to any of this, but then, something clicked in me. Right when her lips touched mine, something clicked, like a switch in my brain.

A tear streamed down my cheek, as I tightened my grasp on the woman's hand, and as I moved my lips in sync with hers.

All of this time, people didn't understand me. They didn't understand what I meant by having someone that I was waiting for, yet not knowing exactly who. Some judged me and ridiculed me. They thought I was just making excuses and wanting to be forever alone.

But, who wants that?

Who wants to not be cared for? Who wants to hide from love?

A while ago, I used to think that I didn't want anyone to worry about me. But, looking at those photos marked with emptiness and lost in time, I realized that that was not it at all.

I wanted someone to worry for me.

I wanted my soul mate...

I slowly opened my eyes, and so, the woman lifted her head up a bit to look at me. Her lips curved into a glorious smile as she stroked my hair. I studied her face, admiring the beauty she had possessed.

The beauty of an angel.

I then cupped my hands around her face as my lower lip began separating from the top.

"You found me..." I breathed.

I felt the emptiness in my heart becoming filled again. For the longest time ever, for all of my life, I had waited for her to find me, to confirm that she was real- that she actually existed.

Katherine leaned closer to me, closing the space between us, as she enveloped me into her warm embrace. I felt the pulse in her veins, as our skin touched, and as our hearts beat as one. I felt her breath on my ear as she then whispered something to me.

"Thanks for remembering me..."